In praise of Susan Emshwiller's writings

Susan Emshwiller's *ALL MY ANCESTORS HAD SEX* is not like anything you have experienced before—unless you're an eighteen-year-old girl named Izzy and have kidnapped your monstrously privileged little brother and driven off in a reconditioned Metro Van to criss-cross the U.S. on a wild road trip, pursued by private eyes, and seeking a way to integrate the fragments of your broken personality. Oh, yes, you'd also have to contend with a half-dozen of your squabbling ancestors, all of whom trail their own tragic histories. In other words, baggage. Find out how Izzy manages to unload it all in this funny and very serious novel—with a heart. Then go and do likewise.

JOHN KESSEL, award-winning author of
The Dark Ride and *The Moon and the Other*

Susan Emshwiller's new novel, I'm happy to say, lives up to its stellar title in every facet. It's a rollicking, rocket's blast chase caper, jammed with rich characters and affecting insights into the human condition. *ALL MY ANCESTORS HAD SEX* delivers a delightfully inventive cross-country thrill ride loaded with surprises and PTSD.

RICHARD KRAUSS editor/publisher of
The Digest Enthusiast

Susan Emshwiller's riveting novel, *ALL MY ANCESTORS HAD SEX*, exploits genealogy as a springboard for a wild, funny, fast-paced tale of misfortune, mayhem, and unlikely redemption. Emshwiller unfolds Izzy's story with such credibility that the reader never doubts the preposterous premises about this 'ugly duckling' daughter of disappointed privileged-class parents. Is this a thriller, a mystery, a romance, a historical novel? Like Izzy herself, it's a little bit of everything. An exhilarating read!!

ANNE ANTHONY, author of
A Blue Moon & Other Murmurs of the Heart

If you are holding this book in your hand, congratulations. If you have chosen to buy this book, chosen from all the books you could have chosen to buy, HUGE CONGRATULATIONS. You are in for a wild and heartfelt ride. What can I say about Susan Emshwiller's writing, except that there is no one like her. She is truly an original.
>
> NANCY PEACOCK, Piedmont Laureate, author of
> *The Life and Times of Persimmon Wilson*

Susan is afraid of nothing in her writing...Full stop. Hilarious! A mother/son fiasco/journey wrapped in love, grit, and impossibility-be- damned!! I promise you will love this wild ride into the inner workings of one whale and one mother.
>
> AMY MADIGAN, actor, producer

Susan Emshwiller wears all her hats in this remarkable and satisfying novel. A page-turner adventure, well-researched and exciting, *THAR SHE BLOWS* is equally as strong for its human drama of a mother and son searching for each other and also themselves. Characters so genuine, flawed, funny and true, they win you over to this improbable premise from the first pages. Enjoy the ride!
>
> GREGG CUSICK, author of
> *My Father Moves Through Time Like a Dirigible*

Remember when you used to get lost in a book, and forget to stop to eat? *THAR SHE BLOWS* is that book. Susan Emshwiller has crafted a romp of a tale about Ann, a woman defined by the color beige, and her 19-year-old, screen-addicted son Brian. When Brian is swallowed by a whale, Ann escapes both her suburban home and her senses in a valiant and delightful journey to rescue him. Make your meals in advance, because once you start reading THAR SHE BLOWS, you're going to want to keep going straight to the end!
>
> MIMI HERMAN, Piedmont Laureate, author of
> *The Kudzu Queen*

A wickedly smart story of a mother losing patience and a son finding direction in the most unusual way possible, *THAR SHE BLOWS* by Susan Emshwiller is a deep dive into the tenderness and tension of mothers and sons. Pushing the literary boundaries of magical realism, this one-of-a-kind novel is a bizarre tale of losing, seeking, and finding...inside the belly of a whale. The tongue-in-cheek prose offsets the serious issues at hand, while the premise teeters perfectly on the brink of allegory, parable, and farce. With whip-smart characters, exceptional comedic timing, and high emotional stakes, this book is a surprising read throughout, balancing an outlandish premise with relatable insight.—SPR

Brush Strokes engages with wit and warmth. Emshwiller sensitively establishes the mystery of a situation, and knows precisely when to sever the action—realizing what needs to be revealed and what doesn't.

Pick of the Week, *LA Weekly*

In *Brush Strokes*...the spectacular results are due to Emshwiller's ingenuity in extracting scenarios ripe with drama. Emshwiller also brings enviable economy and precision to her scripting. There isn't a wasted word in dialogue that reveals entire histories without recourse to expository narration.

Los Angeles Times

A truly original creativity and imagination are apparent throughout *Brush Strokes*. Emshwiller's spare dialogue and virtual absence of exposition—her humor and solid construction skills extend each visual vignetter into a startling, believable and complete mini-play.

Larchmont Chronicle

Emshwiller has—talent, discretion, and affection for her characters.

LA View

Also by Susan Emshwiller

Dominoes - a play

Defrosting Popsicles - a play

Thar She Blows - a novel

All My Ancestors Had Sex - a novel

HOPE IS A THING THAT'S MOLTING

a conglomeration of short writings
by
susan emshwiller

PINEHEAD PRESS

for Mom and Dad
who surrounded us kids with art

HOPE
IS A THING
THAT'S
MOLTING

CONGLOMERATION CONTENTS

SOMETHING BROKE

IT STARTED WITH the sound upstairs. The crash and tinkling of flying bits. His coffee cup? His French press again? No, something lighter. A glass?

In my basement office, I hear curses and sweeping over my head. Broom pushes shards of something.

But I don't get up. I'm not who I was. I don't need to find out and blame and then forgive. I can sit here and be fine.

Whatever broke. I'm fine.

No cup or glass of mine is that crucial. Nothing I can't live without.

I picture all my favorites. The teapot from those six dismal weeks in Eugene. The flea market teacup from France flown back wrapped in underwear. The delicate small vase I use as my end-of-day special glass. The one with the chip on the rim. No matter how I lift it, that chip part ends up at my lips.

Upstairs, the sweeping stops and the shards clatter into the trash. I'm curious, of course. Is it his bear coffee cup, (I know he'd miss that!) or one of the Target candle glasses?

I'm fine. I don't need to look.

Whatever broke, it's nothing important.

Really.

And the morning slinks by. Time for a snack of string cheese and barley tea.

I go up.

He's in his room, so I'm safe to look. But I don't need to. That's childish and vindictive and controlling.

I look under the sink. The garbage is full of food clutter from the drain catches, fruit flies, and paper towels. Nothing broken.

I move to the recycling bin, which is *not* under the sink, which means I'm really totally one hundred percent doing this—going through garbage to FIND OUT SOMETHING.

The recycling bin is full of advertising circulars, Pennysavers, club soda cans, my wine bottle, and shards of something. I pull up a piece. The chipped rim of my favorite glass. My special glass.

Broken.

Remember, I think, *you already imagined this being broken and it was processed and you are ok with being without this glass.*

I remember.

I go downstairs again.

I wonder how he'll tell me.

"Honey, I broke your favorite—"

"I don't know if this was your favorite but—"

"I'm sorry, I broke—"

And the afternoon plods along. He tells me he's going out for groceries. "Burgers for dinner?"

"Ok."

And I can't help myself.

"Have you seen my glass, the one I always use?"

"Which?"

"The vase with the cut designs. I always use it. I can't find it," I lie.

"Haven't seen it," he lies.

And I know I'm forcing the hand and he's not playing and after he leaves I say out loud to myself, "You shouldn't have." And I know that's true.

And the day shambles toward dusk and he returns with dinner and I'm drinking from a DIFFERENT glass than usual and am *somewhat* aloof and waiting.

Just say you broke it, I think. *I'm not your mother. I won't scream and have a tantrum.*

And for once I don't get the mustard and ketchup out for him, although I can't help but toast the buns (even though I don't eat them), because I do them better.

And he gets his own ketchup and mustard and even a plate for me which feels nice and might be a message only I'm eating my burger as a salad and that's why I'm cutting the arugula and iceberg in tiny—tiny—scraps in a BOWL, so he should have noticed and saved the plate.

Halfway through his burger he asks, "Find that glass?"

And I play along saying I haven't and that I even looked in the yard.

And he says how he lost his favorite glass a while back but found it later.

And I nod, pretending that might happen.

And dinner-time drags its feet with the swamp cooler hardly making a dent in the heat because of the humidity.

And after the meal we're both asking "Are you ok?" and "Do you want to talk?" and "It's just the damn heat that's getting us both cranky." And he puts everything away in the fridge but my arugula and blue cheese and iceberg which is okay because they're mine, but he doesn't put away the uncooked leftover hamburger. I allow that maybe he thought I might want more but we already said we were full and that it's hard to eat in this heat and so I get up to put away OUR hamburger meat and something pricks my foot.

I'm barefoot and hopping OW OW and he's asking WHAT? and I know what without looking but I sit and the clear shard of glass is in my heel and I, who am always so annoyingly self-reliant, say, "get it out." And he goes off and, *unlike* usual, I don't fix it before he gets back. I wait and he arrives with a toenail clipper and I remind him we have *tweezers* and I know it sounds bad the second I say it but I can't help it. And he pulls the shard out with the clippers and asks, "OK?"

"It hurts," I answer, just to be mean.

And he leaves to put the WRONG TOOL away and I get up, hobbling some, and start sweeping the kitchen so he'll know I'm STILL WORRIED ABOUT GLASS.

And I know this isn't the best way to deal with things.

And I know he knows that as well.

And he comes back and asks what was in my foot and I say it looked like glass.

And he passes by my broom and dustpan and takes the recycling can out. Takes the evidence out. The front door slams and I hear tinkling glass in the bin outside.

And I know I'm wrong to pretend I don't know and I know he's wrong to pretend he doesn't know and how will we get out of this mess? But I don't say anything. And he doesn't say anything.

And then he's back from the driveway garbage cans and we're talking about the heat and the family and something in the news and all the while it's really about broken glass.

And after a while one of us asks if the other one wants to watch a movie on TV and the other one does, so we set it up, closing the curtains, making beds for the dogs, and settling in to stare at the flickering screen.

And we both pet the dogs and say "There, there," and stare hard at the blue unfolding action, trying to forget about the shards.

And that's the end of the short story.

I write it all out and hand it to him.

"A short story," I say. "It's not *all* totally true. It's for effect. Fiction, you know? Don't get mad."

I go to the living room while he reads at the kitchen table and he coughs twice, then calls me in.

"Fiction, huh?"

"Yep. Well, really only the part about watching TV. I added that to make it more of a story. Like the broken glass is a metaphor for the entire marriage. One of those bleak short short endings."

After that, he says he doesn't know why he lied and I say the same and then I get a tingle and tell him so and we go in and change the draft pattern of the swamp cooler and it doesn't do a bit of good because we end up slippery and sticky and smiling and he can't keep it up and I can't come but we kiss like way-back-when and decide not to end on a bleak short story note.

Someone else can write the bleak short stories. There are too many of them.

And evening dances into night and right now he's out back in his skivvies, checking if our dogs have got skunked and I'm revising this story, turning *No* into *Yes*.

GOOD DOG

When Amelia collapsed in the doorway
and Chris called out "Oh my God,"
I ran in from the bedroom.
She was spayed out flat
and had no heartbeat,
but for a few seconds
her eyes were still with us.
I kept repeating
"Good dog. Good dog,"
knowing that she understood it
and knew it as praise.

When I'm dying
I hope someone will lean close
and hold me
and look into my eyes
and repeat over and over—
if not something just as powerful,
at least
"Good dog."

DINING ALONE ON VALENTINE'S DAY

HER EYES PIERCED ME.

Or she wanted them to.

They fell short and she was left with a feeble glower. No doubt she recognized me from my *Mister Cynical* byline photo. She must have seen my piece opining on the day's occasion and was offended to the core. Readers of my column were always offended. That's why they read me.

She whispered to her dining companion keeping her contemptful glare on me. I'm sure the fact I was flagrantly dining alone on that "Day of Love" was the final affront.

Lacking the verbiage of my occupation, the woman did the only thing she could think of. It was surprisingly poetic.

She pulled the three martini olives off with her teeth and held the pink plastic sword aloft with real bravado. A flick of the wrist and the miniature weapon flew heroically toward my table, hoping to stab my cold heart. It bounced off the white linen, flipped onto my salad plate, and landed beside an abstract expressionist swirl of balsamic vinegar and pomegranate seeds.

I nodded her way as if to accept a compliment. Over the years I'd learned that was the best response to angry fans. Red-faced and tearful, she turned to her companion seeking solace. She probably felt herself a "Romantic" but knew nothing about the root of the movement, only Fairytale love. That disgusted me. That's what my blog on Valentine's day challenged them with.

They thought I was anti-love. Far from it. I was a connoisseur. Take that pretty young exchange student. The Basque. And I did. Both take and bask. One might go so far as to call her a Double Entendre.

No, I certainly had no problem in the love arena. It happened all the time.

"Sir," a boringly trendy busboy hovered over my shoulder, "may I take your plate?"

I retrieved the pink sword and nodded.

When the first one struck just left of my suit tie, I assumed it was another martini sword, but looking for the perpetrator, I saw were her languorous bedroom eyes and the delicate bow of her full moist lips.

Something was amiss because I don't use the word languorous and would never stoop so low as to relate it to eyes. Yet I desired this pandurate beauty more than anyone I'd ever—

Do I know what pandurate means? This was odd—

Number two pricked my left wrist just shy of my faux-lizard-skin Timex. Painful and from an invisible source. These were definitely not via miniature sword attacks. I looked around for the source—the waiter's eyelashes were the longest I'd ever seen. His rippling muscles pressed through that thin white shirt, pulsating with—

Damn it. What was that?! A jab in my cheek and OH MY GOD the most stunning woman slid into the restaurant, all bronzed, tight skin with deep shimmering indigo eyes—Indigo eyes? Really? My words seemed pulled from a trashy romance novel. Was Purple Prose next? Yet even as I had those thoughts, I salivated over the beauty mark beside her vermilion smile, wanting to run my tongue over that delicate mound—OUCH!

Topping off my water, his forearm moved in front of my eyes. Thick and massive. How could I have missed the busboy's sensuality? I fought myself not to lick his skin. His veins bulged on that smooth underside, hints of a tattoo teasing me from his rolled shirtsleeve. If I could undress him—

A whirring by my ear—what was that!?

I spun and at the edge of my vision it darted away, but I'd seen it. The pink cherubic rolls of flesh. The whirring wings. The quivering arrow. I tried to catch another sight but could see nothing except sheep-like diners, paired off as couples, gazing lovingly into each other's eyes. No one seemed to notice the intruders. Surely someone else saw the flashes of pink whizzing overhead.

Was I the only one aware of these creatures? If so, why? Because of my penchant for dining alone on Valentine's Day? Because of my blog on the commercialization of love? Was that a challenge to these little monsters?

Shit. Back of the neck. My mouth opened involuntarily as my eyes absorbed the magnificence of her. She of the martini sword. The bounty of her flesh. The rolls gently bouncing in rhythm to her tinkling laughter. The effervescence of corporality she exuded—

Whirring of wings by my ear—I did the whip-the-tablecloth-from-under-the-dishes-trick but it was less than successful and the china and glass shattered as I swirled the linen overhead. There was a little "oo!" and I knew one of them was hit, so I swung the cloth high and twisted back quickly and got the thing trapped and pressed to the table. Stabbing pricks hit me from all sides. There must be a dozen of the—God she was lovely—his chest—her feet!—that curve in the small—just made out his bulge—

I held the pink martini sword against the wriggling mass within the cloth and when I pressed that little weapon just a bit a muffled voice sang out an unintelligible stream of vowels. The onslaught of pricks stopped.

I was having trouble focusing. The Maître d' was stunning. His mustache so thin. Touching it would be like tracing a velvet skein of Arabian cashmere. I wondered what his Adam's apple did when—

More vowels from the squirming form in the table cloth bundle.

The other patrons were staring. Staring at a lanky man standing over his table holding an miniature sword to an unseen mass and looking the part of a flash mob participant with the wrong address.

"Sir, is there a problem?" the Maître d' asked.

I pressed on the creature under the cloth and did a head tilt that hopefully meant—*Yes there is a problem, don't you see the squirming thing I caught?*

The Maître d' sniffed disdainfully. His Arabian cashmere mustache now lay like a rat tail hot-glued to his upper lip and it stretched as he gestured toward the kitchen, "Shall we, sir?"

Gathering my writhing bundle, I followed the Maître d' into the kitchen, all the way hearing the murmur of confused patrons, curses from blog subscribers, and the fluttering of wings overhead.

In the bright room, the Chef glared at the intrusion. His bushy eyebrows crashed into each other like challenging bulls. As the Maître d' turned to me, I heard the release of many tiny arrows from many tiny bows, yet I felt nothing. Not one prick.

That rat-tail mustache curved up into a smile shape and the Chef's bull-brows parted and rose and I knew those two had been hit. They were in love with me. I became the most magnificent thing they'd ever seen. Such adulation I'd never experienced. It gave me pause, but I knew it wasn't about me. There was a war afoot and the winged ones intended to win.

I had other plans. "You've lobster on the menu tonight?" I asked.

The Chef blushed, shaking with desire for me. He couldn't speak so shyly pointed to the huge pot of boiling water.

I slipped the pink body out from the cloth and saw only a flash but his baby blue eyes sparked angrily and his arrow rose, bow arching and I tipped him into the pot—

The scream was high and made us hunch and the fluttering others vanished in a whir and the boiling overtook the desperate flapping of cupid's wings.

That was twenty years ago.

I understand that several patrons met their life partners that night after eating the unusual "amuse-bouche." I left before he was carved and haven't fallen in love since.

This poem is from a dream. In the dream I saw this entire poem printed in a book.

OF BANISHING FEAR

It works for all forms of fear.

Have the patient lay naked,
face down on a soft white sheet.
Tell them to keep their eyes closed.

Tell them, "The wolves will come but
when is never predictable.
Sometimes one wolf,
sometimes two."
Then leave.

The wolves come down roaring.
They race along the sides of the body
around the arm pits,
down over the thighs,
howling and snapping,
rolling with growls and stiff hair and dirty claws.

They leap and disappear,
then one jumps back,

landing hard, as a surprise.
The other gets an old rusty pick-up truck
and drives along the patient's back,
dipping behind the knees,
rumbling over cracked soles,
skidding on wrinkled elbows.
Not to be outdone, the other wolf gets his truck
and bounces over crevices and mounds
and jutting shoulder blades,
tangling hair in tires
and gunning the motor too loud.

After leaving red circling skid marks
all over the patient's skin
the two wolves abandon their trucks
and take to leaping surprise attacks again.

The moments between attacks
get longer
and
longer
until
both wolves stay up
as stars
and one never knows
if
or when
they'll pounce again
but the patient's fear is gone.

Usually, all the dazed patient can whisper
is the word
"grateful."

SUICIDE WATCH

MASON DOESN'T LOOK like a loser. Blue eyes. Blond hipster cut. College age. He looks like someone I'd hang out with. But doing this, he's gotta be a loser.

I don't know if I can handle being here. Will I barf? It's all new and I'm shaking, fingering the Panic Clicker in my pocket.

He lifts the gun's barrel to his forehead and mouths something but no sound comes out. No wonder the dude is offing himself.

There's a loud *BANG* and he flies back and horror rushes through me and sadness and something like guilt and then —shivering glee.

I'm so pumped!

I feel!

There's lots of jitters and I do barf and sit kinda crying on the edge of the tub and when I can stand, there I am in the mirror, wide-eyed and a mess. Blood and bits of bone and brain spatter me. Next time I'll wear a raincoat and goggles. *Next time. Ha! That didn't take long. My first one down and already there's a next time.*

The buzzer sounds and the glass door slides open, welcoming me into the Death Tours™ tasteful lobby. Behind the thick glass separating us, Simone, the receptionist, presents a TV smile but her eyes don't join the effort.

"I'm here for another tour," I try to say causally. My fourth. I hope she's not counting.

"Certainly, sir. You have a preference or shall we let Fate decide?"

"I think Fate this time."

"Wonderful. Time frame?"

"Let's make it in a few hours."

"Not longer? No backstory?"

I shake my head. "Don't want to lose the suspense."

"Sex preference?"

I twist my mouth like I'm deciding now. "Hmmm. Let's go with a female."

"Certainly. Credit card?"

"Visa."

A signature and Simone offers her smile again. "We'll be contacting you shortly."

She puts the Panic Clicker in the mini-revolving-door thingy, spins it through to my side, and we're done.

Everything's so much more visceral when you know. It's like you see the gum spots on the sidewalk sharper. The coffee shop smell hits harder. The music of the Puerto Rican delivery boys almost sounds good as it rises from the open cellars. Everything in the city feels vividly exciting.

I step down from the sidewalk to my basement apartment. Stinks down here. Some bum must have peed by my door again.

No message on my phone or email. They must not have gotten a call yet.

The microwave nukes chicken nuggets. It spins and I imagine my Host, whoever she is. She's wondering if it's worth it. She's wondering if there might be a better place. She's wondering if it will hurt. She could be the next block over, nuking her a last supper. Is she thinking about me, her Witness?

I'm so excited I can barely get down one chicken nugget.

TV's smiling colors blast me. There's that reality star. I used to like her, but now Reality TV can't hold a candle to Reality Life. These tours are so personal. One of a kind. Only *I* get to see the end. *I'm* the one in the know. Not half the world.

My phone shimmies on the coffee table. That's got to be the tour.

I wait for the shimmy to stop and the voicemail to ping.

"Valued Customer, your tour is about to start. Please proceed to East Fifteenth—"

I tap the address into my phone. Map says six subway stops and a short walk.

Jeans and a T should be fine. Since it's a girl, I don't imagine I'll need my raincoat and goggles. Girls don't like to make messes.

Rush hour already. Sidewalks packed. Bumping off people, their faces lit by phones. Heading down the stairs into the subway, a young man rises toward me. Blood speckles his skin and shirt. Eyes full of adrenaline and the sly smile of accomplishment. We pass with a nod of recognition.

I step down to the subway station. All these anonymous faces are no longer boring. Any one of them could be a participant. That dude near the edge of the platform. He's over the yellow line. A Host? Another guy watches behind him. The Witness? There's the man in the beige jumpsuit, trying to be unobtrusive. The Facilitator. Definitely a Death Tour™. I stare at the Witness. He glances up at me, then turns back quickly, focusing on the dude by the edge. He's got his game-head on. Guy has to be pissed it'll be in public. Everyone can watch. Not so special.

The air in the tunnel shifts and swirls my hair. Sound grows. The Witness moves his weight from leg to leg unconsciously. Anxious. The dude over the yellow line doesn't move. No drama. He knows what happens next.

Garbage blows up from the tracks as the train races in and the dude over the yellow line makes a move. A tilt. If you weren't looking, you'd miss it. A tilt and he's gone. The Witness rushes forward, breathless. His face flushes with emotion. He's probably followed this guy for a day or more. He starts sobbing. Feels something at last.

The train rattles to a stop and although we all want to see what's left on the tracks, the cleanup crew herds us inside, leaving the Witness his prize. We crane to see the man's face, each of us hoping for a second-hand feeling. No such luck. The train pulls us away.

Six stops and I'm out. The street lights buzz on.

Two short blocks, step up the stoop, and push the button for Apartment 12 E. No one answers. I better not have missed the action. Refund will be in order. I push and hold the button.

The buzzer sounds and I pull open the front door. It must be weird for her to buzz me in.

The elevator shudders to the twelfth floor. The hall is narrow and smells of mold. A bored-looking Facilitator straightens, checks my I.D. with his tablet, and nods me to the apartment. 12 E's door is ajar.

Dark room. She's sitting in front of the window, silhouetted by the orange city glow. Her head makes a movement like she's heard me enter, but she knows enough not to look directly at me. It's so much better when they don't look. I can pretend to be invisible.

My phone shines blue as I hold it up but I make sure to turn off the flash. Of course we can film and upload to YouTube, but I prefer to post one or two pics and keep the rest for myself. I'll have seen something no one else has.

She turns on the small lamp by the table. A jolt of surprise shoots through me. She can't be more than twenty and some Asian kind of beautiful. Dark straight hair hangs low, hiding the nipples that might be showing through her sheer T-shirt. She's either a starving refugee, anorexic, a model, or all of the above.

She rises stiffly and pauses at the microwave. Punches numbers. The whirring starts. Smells of something ethnic. An exotic unpleasant tartness. I hope she won't start talking in a language I can't understand. Or write a final note in some script with slashes and curlicues and no normal letters.

The machine beeps *done.* She lifts the carton, clearly burning the fingers holding it, but now that she's on view, she doesn't want to show pain or fear. She better not be drugged so she won't feel anything. How am I supposed to feel if she doesn't? I'll demand a refund if that turns out to be the case.

She's using chopsticks like no wannabe can. Slurping, even. Looks like the same ramen noodles we all eat, but with authentic ingredients that make it smell like a horse stable.

My stomach growls. Her slurping stops. I should have eaten more chicken nuggets.

The girl pulls another ramen container from the cupboard, peels back the plastic, adds faucet water, and sticks it in the microwave. *Whir . . .* She goes back to her slurping.

I've got a terrible feeling she's acknowledging I'm here. No, she's hungry. She's been starving herself and now, before she ends it, she's going to pig out with two ramens.

Glancing at my phone, I get her info. *Janet.* She doesn't look like a Janet. I'll give her a name that suits her. Exotic. Oriental. Hibachi. Toyota. Mitsubishi. Seiko.

Seiko.

Seiko takes the second ramen from the microwave, sets it on the table with another pair of chopsticks, and walks past me. Stepping into the bathroom, she turns on the light and pulls the door, leaving it ajar 'cause we're allowed total access.

The horse-stable ramen steams. I don't suppose it would be against any rules if I helped myself. I'm paying enough.

I never got the hang of chopsticks. I shine my phone into the drawer for a fork.

The ramen has a dark taste, more swamp than I care for, but I suck it down and drink the broth before I hear the flush.

Seiko comes from the bathroom and takes her and my carton away without seeming to notice that there are two empty containers. I almost want to thank her, but that would screw everything up. She's got her job to do and I'm here to watch.

She sits in front of the window and turns out the lamp, looking down to the street. Sirens howl as usual. Lights in the apartment across the way go on. I move near. I want to see what she's seeing so I can feel what she's feeling.

The glow of the city shines on the tabletop, on her thin wrists—one of them banded by a thick bracelet. I stare until I can see her pulse tapping under the skin. I wonder if she'll use these wrists as part of the finale. They are so smooth. I hope it won't be pills. I've been through that and it is BORING. You can't even tell when it's over.

She taps her phone and super-sad violin music starts. The classic sob-story piece. Second time I've heard it this month. The notes mourn all around us and Seiko looks out at the city and all the lives and the heavy strings cry and we'll never be enough or do enough and why can't it ever get better?

I let my tears dribble down and wet my collar rather than moving to wipe them away. She probably knows she's making me cry. That's a triumph of a sort.

Seiko lifts her thin arm and waves to the lit apartments. Does that mean someone else is watching her? Is my Tour getting diluted? I'm supposed to be the only one! As she keeps waving, I see the tear roll down her cheek. She wants to say goodbye to this last day, this last hour, this last minute. That's so moving!

Tap. Tap. Tap.

Tap—Tap—Tap—

Tap. Tap. Tap.

She's doing a Morse code thing on the table with her long fingernails.

No one knows Morse code but everyone knows SOS. It means Danger. Distress. Help. What's the deal? She's not asking for help, is she? I'm not here for that. I'm not here to save anyone. I paid a bundle for Suicide Watch.

Seiko opens her mouth, but stops herself from speaking. She aims a finger at a Band-Aid at the tender crook of her elbow. Did she already cut herself? Shoot up with drugs? I'm supposed to see it all. A swift pull strips the bandage away revealing pen scrawls on her skin. I move close to read it. She smells of something pink. The scrawled words read: *The House always wins.*

What's that supposed to mean? Sounds like a judgment. Better not be about me. I'm not keen on someone spouting shit about life and my role and consumerism and all that. She better not be a spouter. My fingers run over the Panic Clicker in my pocket.

Seiko walks to the door in a *let's get this show on the road* move.

In the hall, as we pass the waiting Facilitator, he averts his eyes, acknowledging my exclusive viewing privileges. I follow Seiko up the stairs, pretending that I don't exist. My footsteps echo in the stairwell. We climb up three flights, push open the heavy door, and step onto the roof.

Seiko is more businesslike than I want right now. She's not weeping or looking weak. She steps to the edge of the building. The wind kicks up her shirt. She is thin!

I move to her side so I won't miss anything. I need to see her face and all of her expressions.

She takes a deep breath, inhaling the city for the last time. The soot. The diesel. The cooked grease. Festering garbage. Rot of the Hudson.

She turns her head, listening. A dog cries somewhere. Footsteps on the street. A television. Sirens. Thousands of air conditioners in thousands of windows. A foghorn from the river. I didn't realize we were so close to the water. The lights of the bridge wink and shimmy in the swift current. Green neon dances upside down in black waves.

Seiko steps onto the ledge. The clothes around her shake. She is terrified. Joy tingles over me. This is what is so magical about life. It scares you to lose it. There must be something to it after all.

She turns, looking right at me. I don't want to be looked at but I can't turn away.

And then—

Wind pulls at me as she drops. I lean over, watching the thin limbs twist and struggle to find something other than air. Each gesture captured like a fashion shoot. The hair spreading. The shirt lifting. The ankle bent just so.

The sidewalk stops her with a cracking thud. I zoom my phone to take pics but the flash won't work from this distance. Need to be closer. I start down the stairwell to get my money's worth, but my eyes blur and I only make it to her floor. The Facilitator is already gone. I wonder how he knew.

Sitting in Seiko's dark apartment, I relive her last moments—tap S . . . O . . . S . . . on her table and wave slowly, while the cleaning crew hoses down the street.

I wake in my apartment to my friends. My friends are generally from the cable channels; the locals don't interest me. Occasionally I'll spend time with some newcomer, a new weather girl, or during the award season I'll pay particular attention to the hot chicks in the commercials, but I like the steady relationships best. Shows with many seasons. You get to know them and care about them.

I sort Seiko's pics, post two to my page. Pings from *Likes* come in as I send the best pic to the printer. She was pretty. I wonder if we would have gotten along if circumstances had been different. Probably. She could have taught me to use chopsticks.

Her pic goes on the wall next to Mason, Fraizer, and Camille. Four total. I should stop. Seiko's a good one to go out with. But if I stop I'll have to do something else to feel. Go to a museum and look at art? They say it moves people, makes them feel things, but I doubt it can compete with a Suicide Watch.

My phone beeps. 11:00. *Morning with Ginny.* I flip to the Weather Channel and she comes on bright and hot and floods my room with her smile.

Three weeks and eleven suicides later, I step into Death Tours™ but receptionist Simone doesn't offer the smile I've been paying for. She explains. I'm tapped out. Overextended. There will be no more jolts to prove I'm alive if I don't fix my finances.

Simone retrieves the smile that's packed away and assures me there is a solution.

"We have a special credit plan for our Valued Customers, whereupon you are able to access all Death Tours™ has to offer without the hindrance of financial stress. Shall I show you that option?"

With my nod, Simone pushes a button and the contract appears, projected onto the thick glass between us. Miles of words.

"I get to continue?" I ask.

"Click the AGREE box and we're all set."

I touch the glass, the AGREE box shines bright as the words vanish, and I schedule my next Suicide Watch.

After the Facilitator checks my I.D., he steps aside and I knock. Ansel's maybe fourteen but big for his age. He lets me into the loft and turns his back, hunching over something, probably preparing his method. I hope it's not a gun. I'm not in the mood. There's a noose hanging from the ceiling pipes. Good. Haven't seen a hanging yet.

I slide around to check what he's up to and he spins, raising the black shape to his face. The flash of his camera blinds me and, as the ancient Polaroid spits a photo to the ground, he dives, ramming me into the window. He's at me, fists everywhere. I hunch and struggle to get the Panic Clicker from my pocket.

Ansel punches my nose and *snap* and I'm on the matted rug and face-to-face with the developing Polaroid—me looking like a red-eyed dork.

Spin and kick and backwards-crab-scramble—grab something—a glass jar full of whatever—it's up and down hard, shattering over Ansel's head, scattering shards and Polaroids of other red-eyed dorks—and I'm thinking, *All those people are dead.*

Ansel shakes glass from his hair and I've got my Panic Clicker out and what was the procedure? *Remove cover. Press red activation button. High whistling tone as it charges. Green light means Fire.*

I flip the cover and Ansel looks like he knows. Bet he's one like me.

His fist to my stomach and elbow around my neck, dragging me backwards toward the noose.

I imagine my feet dancing in the air.

No.

This is not *my* death. This is *yours.*

I wrench my body and slam him hard. He falls and three smashes to his eye and he's chilled for now and I push the Panic Clicker button and the high whine starts and he's cringing but I don't care because *three, two, one—green and FIRE.*

White sparks crackle on his chest and he jerks around like the goldfish I had as a kid. I used to watch it flop in my hand and only put it back in the water when it started to slow. Mom never got why my fish kept dying.

Ansel's mouth opens in a scream but he must hurt bad 'cause only air comes out.

A pounding on the door. Got to be the Facilitator.

"Everything's fine!" I yell.

My phone tingles. A text. *Panic Clicker. Situation?*

I text back. *Situ resolved. All clear.*

Hell, I sound like I know what I'm doing.

My nose throbs so I reactivate my Clicker. High whistling. Light turns green. I zap Ansel's ankle. He does another air scream as black char lines spider across his bare skin where the electricity scattered.

It gives me a jolt. This might not be a bad way to get feelings—*engineering* other people to feel things rather than only watching.

More door-pounding. "Do you need facilitation?"

"NO! Stop intruding on my Tour!"

I glare at Ansel and gesture to the noose.

He watches me recharge the Clicker and nods. It must hurt that much.

Drags a chair below the noose and steps up. Pulls the knot tight behind his neck, a thick bracelet on his wrist. I've seen that before.

Mouth flops like a video on mute. Blue tongue.

Ansel takes the step off. His feet kick and flail and search for the chair, but I help by pulling it out of reach. His face gets puffy and red. Eyes bulge and, meeting mine, I'm feeling it. The loss. The terror. The fear.

The high whistle of the Clicker and *Green* and *Fire*. Electricity wakes him. Eyes red. He makes the scream face.

Pounding on the door.

High whistle and *Green* and *Fire*. Veins swell on his forehead.

Pounding.

Green and *Fire*. Red spit flies from his blue mouth.

Feet slow and twitch. Eyes still.

The pounding outside stops.

Another text: *Facilitation needed?* I respond: *Panic Clicker malfunction. All fine.*

Ansel swings in smaller and smaller arcs.

After a while, the Clicker doesn't charge any more. Ran out of juice.

My phone snaps a pic of me and Ansel. Well, me and his torso. I hold the lens lower and point up. This time it gets Ansel hanging and my head at the bottom. No matter. When I post it, people will know I had an experience. One no one else had.

Back at my pad, I get a lot of *Thumbs-ups* and *Likes*.

As I stick a printed blowup of Ansel on my memento wall with the others, the text comes in: *Call Death Tours™ Credit Department.*

I do and the call confirms the worst. Death Tours™ gives me a choice. Pay or Play. There's no way I can pay what I owe. The next suicide has to be my own.

My Suicide Watches stare down from the wall. Were they *all* like me—witnesses till their credit ran out? I should have stopped but it was the only thing that penetrated the dullness of living. Now I have to kill myself?

No. I won't do it. I'll run away. Take a subway somewhere.

Knocking on the door. The peephole shows a beige jumpsuit with the Death Tours™ logo. That was fast. I'll play along like I'm planning to go through with it so they won't suspect. I undo the dead bolts and chain and open to the Facilitator. He checks my name and face against his tablet.

"For your convenience, I'm here to facilitate the scheduling. We have a few options available."

It's a lot different scheduling my own suicide. Death Tours™ doesn't give flexibility like when you're a Valued Customer. Eight or nine tonight are my only options. I choose nine.

The day goes fast and the Facilitator stays outside my door. I hope it still stinks of pee out there.

I think and think and can't come up with a plan. It's almost eight. I've got the TV on to distract me but that's not working. If this is really gonna happen, who will be my Witness? What if it's some jerk who slurps soda and munches popcorn while watching me? Or what if he does instant streaming and I can hear the *likes* ping in. What if they aren't *likes*? What if it's *thumbs-downs*?

As the TV program changes, there's a knock at the door. That's not right. It's an hour early.

I peek out to see the large chest of the Facilitator. He knocks again.

Chain still on the door, I undo the dead bolts.

"Left hand, sir."

He clamps a thick band around my offered wrist. It doesn't look like the kind of thing you can remove on your own.

"Monitors vitals, et cetera."

"Et cetera?"

"Should the Death Tour™ not proceed as contracted, the band emits a fast-acting subcutaneous solution."

This is becoming way too real.

Pulling a clear container from his pocket, he offers me a blue ball. "Think of it as candy. Suck on it until it's all dissolved. No chewing."

I take the sucker and start to close the door.

"Suck it now. I have to confirm completion."

"What does it do?" I ask.

"Numbs the tongue and vocal cords. Prevents unwanted interactions." He gestures for me to get sucking.

It tastes more red than blue. Red with background chemicals. Like drinking cherry soda in a disinfected public toilet.

It feels creepy to have this man watch me suck hard candy but the way he looks I don't dare swallow early. Tongue out to show him it's gone and he marks the tablet and steps back from the door. No *goodbye*, or *good luck*, or *bon voyage*.

Dead bolts flipped.

There's got to be some way out of this, only I can't think of one. This is not fun. I need a plan. Problem is, with this bracelet and its fast-acting sub-whatever-solution, I may be out of options.

I don't like this.

8:45. Fifteen minutes until my final Death Tour™. I activate the internal camera on the big computer. My face fills the screen.

Shit. Look at me.

I look scared. I look like all those others. Terrified of ending it.

Gives me a thrill.

Not recording, I set my phone in selfie mode. Switch my tablet to camera view. Now I've got my image across three screens.

This is fantastic. The thumping in my chest revs to overdrive.

Guy in the screens sticks out his tongue. Blue! Ha! Good one!

The razor blade at my wrist goes in easy. Stings but the view in the screens is fantastic. He's panting and wide-eyed. It's so real. Like watching and feeling at the same time. The ultimate show.

Cut below the thick bracelet. Red flowing down my arms. I gasp goldfish-like.

A pounding on the door. Ha. Those suckers will be too late.

Peer out my basement window. View of feet and tires and pigeons pecking at black gum on the sidewalk. Look into the glowing night and wave like Seiko did. Everything is shimmery and magical. There's something about a Suicide Watch that makes life feel . . . alive.

Pounding's drifting into noiselessness.

My sixteen Death Tours™ memento pics look down on me. Shit! I need my photo up there. Just one. No one gets to see anything else.

FLASH and send to computer. My sliced wrists hurt and there is definitely something loosening in me. Like I'm losing reception.

Push *Print*.

Bloody fingerprints on the picture but it's up with the others.

That's some grin. Fucker fucked them. You *can* beat the House.

I turn to the face in the screens and he's almost beautiful. I try to say good job, but no sound comes out. Oh well. I know what I meant.

Look at the screens. He's fading.

And only I get to see. Only me.

MUSIC THEORY

MR. BOWER pulled the white handkerchief from his suit pocket. It was the bottom of the eighth period and the cloth had lost all its starched creases.

He wiped the sweat from his upper lip. The afternoon sun was blasting in but he wasn't going to take off his jacket. Never had and wasn't going to start today.

Rubbing the cotton cloth as he slipped it back in his pocket, he wondered if she would still iron these every evening after dinner? What would they do after dinner if he didn't have to grade papers and she didn't have to set out tomorrow's suit? Was that the change she'd spoken about?

Bach's Cantata 140 Sleepers Awake played. The sixteen-year-olds all had their heads bowed. Not in reverence. Not listening. But they were not bored. Mr. Bower and Bach were irrelevant. Grubby fingers were busy tapping out secret messages to be sent from one classroom to another. From one desk to another. At first Mr. Bower had insisted the devices be turned off, but the effort proved too great. Now he simply did his job as background noise.

Mr. Bower pushed Pause. Granted, the digital contraption provided a small fraction of convenience, but those heavy record players and carefully cleaned albums had given him a sense of pride. He had played those same grooves for years. Scores of children had seen him lift the needle arm and deftly lower it one thirty-second of an inch shy of the end of the track, hitting the mark perfectly, five or so bars before the resolution.

This digital thing involved no skill.

"As you can hear," Mr. Bower intoned, raising his voice as if he was still in the past when children were unruly and chattered loudly to each other. This class was silent, preoccupied with their ubiquitous devices. "As you can hear, Bach dances around the melody and we arrive here. The obligatory passage to Home. The tonic."

No face turned up to him. Some of the younger teachers tried to connect to their pupils with pop music, but Mr. Bower frowned upon such coddling. He was sticking to The Masters.

"And you will notice the retard."

Several heads looked up, snickering. That never failed.

"The retard at the end, the slowing of the tempo to draw out that delicious tension as we wait to arrive at the tonic. Delicious tension. Anticipation of pleasure. No doubt, some of you may be old enough to have a enjoyed a physical corollary to this sensation."

No reaction. Obtuse halfwits.

Maybe if he had gone along with her wishes he might feel differently toward the pimply, slouching rabble before him. Maybe if they had taken one of those babies when it was clear she couldn't get pregnant. But he couldn't see raising someone else's child and now it was much too late.

"What is the tonic? Home. The resting place where all feels complete and resolved."

That red haired boy looked up. Could it be he's interested? Perhaps the child was from a broken home and the idea of resolution appealed to him.

No, the boy was looking at the clock. Kid probably had his phone confiscated by some more dedicated teacher. Someone who hadn't given up. The boy wanted to know when class would end. Mr. Bower had no need to check the time. He was infinitely aware of Time; how it slid past silently but with an ever increasing *accelerando*. Mr. Bower knew the bell would ring in five minutes.

It was almost over. *Tell them about home*, he reminded himself.

Mr. Bower pushed Play. The notes cascaded and tumbled and danced and teased and slowed to that moment—he licked his lips—slowed to that moment—wait for it, please let it happen—and—then it did. The tonic. Home. Resolution.

Mr. Bower looked at his pupils. No one in the stuffy classroom cared.

"Each key in our diatonic scale, what you undoubtedly know as Do, Ra, Me, Fa, So, La, Ti—"

He let the 7th note hold in the air. No one responded.

"Anyone?"

That Rubio boy said, "Doe a deer. A female deer."

The class laughed.

A jolt of something burped up in Mr. Bower. A flash of rage and excitement.

"Yes, exactly."

Mr. Bower stepped to the piano. He was tempted to play his favorite Chopin Grande Valse Brillante in E-flat major Op. 18 to show he could have been so much more than a high school teacher. He could have had a career. Or at least given lessons to individual students, motivated students, rather than this endless parade of riff-raff. His finger hovered over the key, then tapped out the opening, the quick B flat notes, and he realized he hadn't played in years. He no longer knew what came next. It was in his head, but not in his hands. He only knew the idea, the theory, not the actual practice.

Is this what she had meant when she'd said he wasn't part of the marriage anymore? When she'd said he wasn't playing anything but scales?

A slight catch jerked his heart. Was it really that bad?

No, it would all work out. If nothing else, he could count on her. He could always count on her. He tapped the B flat again.

Give them the theory. At least they might feel the music, he thought.

Looking out at his audience he started a half step higher at "Middle C. Doe," singing along as his fingers stepped upward, "Re, Me, Fa, So, La, Ti—"

He hit the Ti note several times.

A few heads looked up, annoyed.

"Yes, you had to look. Why? Because it's the LEADING note. The 7th. You know the key and are waiting for the *resolution*. The tonic. Home."

He hit the 7th five more times.

"See how you long for the resolution? It is anguish not to get it. Musical torture."

Three more times on the B and the bell rang, disturbingly not a C.

The class rose en masse clattering out and by the end of the ringing the room was empty.

Mr. Bower paused, then quietly touched the C. Resolution.

And that was the end of it. The last period of the last day of the last semester of the last year. His job was over. The end.

What was the point? None of his students would ever remember any of it. It had nothing to do with their lives. Unlike some of his colleagues, in his 35 years of teaching not one student had ever returned to visit him. He had never been slipped a note of appreciation. He'd never heard of any child going on to pursue a musical career. Was it his failure?

Mr. Bower closed the piano lid. There was no reason to look around the room one last time. It was as it had always been. He would see it forever. He lifted his overcoat from the hook, stepped out into the crowded hall, locked the room, and out of habit put the ring of keys in his pocket, took two steps toward the glare of the doors and then turned back the other way.

In the main office, Mrs. Shiff smiled as he handed her the keys. He could see she wanted to say something to him. Some words of comfort or praise or conclusion, but he shook his head and waved her silent and left the office for the hall. Left the hall for the door. Left the school for good.

The usual chaos was even more so. End-of-the-school-year energy. Mr. Bower walked through the excited throng, crossing the parking lot. Several teachers were standing together, talking with that same start-of-summer excitement. They waved at him and he nodded, turning away so they wouldn't feel obligated to invite him over.

At the light, he had to stand with a crowd of children. Their squeals and laughs were grating. More than usual. Crossing the street someone banged into him and kept moving. Rage surfaced again. How he had pressed it down all these years? Never let his voice rise in anger in that classroom. But he knew it leaked out. It leaked out with her. On her.

She had told him things needed to change. She said it again this morning when she'd helped him on with his coat. He had nodded as usual, but not responded. Of course, things would change. There would be none of that familiar routine. No tests to grade. No lesson plans to create. No music to assemble. No bratty children with snotty attitudes to tell her about. All of that would be gone. They would have to find new routines to fill the time.

A car honked. Two tones smashed together in dissonance. Mr. Bower winced. An uneasy feeling was rising in his stomach. A bile.

She hadn't kissed him goodbye at the door. He had been in too much of a hurry to notice then, but now the memory of it set him on edge. Last night she had wanted to talk about their next stage, but he'd dismissed her, wanting to focus on the final lesson.

His pace quickened as he crossed the park. An accelerando of the tempo. The beat of his heart.

Perhaps all this time he had missed the signs. Ignored the words. Thought he knew the theme, but missed the evolving variations.

He knew now. He saw it. He used to play Chopin and Schumann and even Oscar Peterson for her. But that was long ago. He had been playing only scales for longer than he could remember. There was no reason she would be there. The house would be empty. Having him around all day would be unbearable for her. She will have packed.

Mr. Bower started trotting. He imagined the silence in the living room. The silence in the bedroom. The ticking clock loud in the empty kitchen. She'll have left a note, but with no way to reach her.

Panic grabbed his gut. He was no longer Mr. Bower, he was Bert and he was terrified. How would he live without her?

Bert hadn't run in years. It was hard and jarring. His belly bounced. His ankles felt weak and something caught his foot and he stumbled. The sidewalk zoomed in front of his eyes and his hands caught it as his knees hit hard. Bert felt a rush of tears but pushed himself up and hobbled forward. Their house was now only a block away. He didn't want to know. What if he ran past and never knew? Would he be able to live if he opened the door on emptiness?

Up the driveway. Why didn't they have windows in the garage door? He would have been able to look in and know.

Bert reached his scraped hand into his coat pocket and saw himself give his keys to Mrs. Shiff. He hadn't removed the house key. He was locked out.

A whining in his ear. A high pitched sound. He turned the doorknob. Yes, it was locked. He wouldn't be able to enter the abandoned house. He wouldn't be able to see the note. He couldn't go back to school for the keys. Not now. Not like this.

Tingling rushed over him as he heard a sound. A sound from inside. The door lock turning.

A curdling in his body. His mouth opened. Every nerve reached out to hear—to see—the anticipation spread over him and pressed around his throat and groin.

The knob rotated and he felt that moment of time stretch. The holding of the 7th. The leading tone aching—

And her face was there, wide and familiar, smiling as he pulled her close and his heart brimmed with arriving. Brimmed with joy and peace. The resolution. Tonic. Home.

GRANDMA'S MIRROR

Amidst the uproar of boxes
I found and unpacked
the treasured
hand-held golden mirror of my Grandmother.
"Mir-a-gold" etched in the worn metal handle.
Probably a first-year anniversary present
from her one-armed husband
ordered thru the Montgomery Ward
or Sears Roebuck catalogue.

Monogramed with SBE.
Susie B Emshwiller.
The B standing for nothing more
than the desire to have a middle initial
for this mirror.
So I've been told.

Here, in the strange new house—
from her era actually—
where all is out-of-place
and frighteningly unfamiliar,
I find my Grandmother's mirror
and hold it up—
and Lo—

there's my face!
My familiar face.

I hadn't packed it,
yet it made the trip.
Looking a little dazed,
but intact.

AFTER CHRISTMAS TURKEY

"THE HELL YOU SAY! Never could 'afore and ain't gonna now," Uncle Walter screams over the blaring football game.

"We'll see what's what," Uncle Max yells. "Get your ass to the table!"

"Max! The children!" Aunt Eullie scolds as the uncles slam their walkers away from the television.

My wife glares at me and steps to the bathroom for the fifteenth time.

"Your Jenny have that irritable bowel syndrome?" Grandma Winchell asks loudly, spitting scalloped potato onto my wrist and setting up the twins to squeal "Bowel, bowel!" on endless repeat. "She's going too often for a healthy soul. I'm past ninety and you don't see me traipsing to the powder room every five minutes. Or is it true, what they say?"

"What's that Grandma?" I ask as the uncles bumper-car their walkers closer.

"Are you city people always taking the cocaine?"

I open my mouth like I'm laughing and get up, clearing her plate.

The Uncles dump themselves at the gravy spill corner of the table. Uncle Max pushes back the poinsettia which causes someone's wine glass to tip over, mixing with the gravy. Drips of the gooey concoction trickle to the floor and Vivian's Pomeranians rush to lap the treat.

The Uncles start arm wrestling, mumbling and cursing their well-rehearsed play.

Wish I could still drink. This is hell without booze. Gathering slime-covered plates, I step toward the kitchen.

"Gotta pay the toll," Little Tiffany says, blocking my way, iPhone held high. She sees I'm clueless and says, "Look up."

Mistletoe. Shit.

At fifteen, Little Tiffany isn't little anymore. Gramma Alice would call her a Harlot.

I bend to plant a kiss on her chee—*DAMN!*—her tongue flicks into my mouth and FLASH goes the camera. Me jerking back, Tiffany skipping away fiddling with the phone, I spin and smash into—*that new wife had the cancer—Patricia!*—her bowl of baked-something and my dishes rise —then descend. Everything breaks. Wads of marshmallow and green jello fly.

"My ambrosia!" Patricia screams.

Flecks dot my corduroy pants. Too bad they didn't make it as far as the snowmen and reindeer frolicking across my belly.

From the cold vestibule Mother snarls, "What the hell, Mark!" her Camel clenched in her teeth, breathing verboten nicotine fumes into the kitchen.

"Grandma! The baby's lungs!" Jeanette, or Jeanine, cries.

Mother snuffs the cigarette in her eggnog. "You go to Kroger's and get a replacement desert, Mark. Ice cream. But none of that commie kissy-kissy druggy liberal-agenda Vermont ice cream. Get Nestle, Oreos, and Coolwhip."

Thank God! I can leave!

"And take my handicap sign for your car. You can park close."

"I don't need it, Mother."

"Take it. Might be the only place to park if the store is full of idiots like you shopping to replace the deserts they broke!" She waves the wheelchair logo sign in front of my face, creating a welcome breeze.

I don't even bother telling my wife where I'm going. Get in the car. One block away, the Stones on full blast to drown out the voices in my head. *I can't do another three days of this!*

Slam gearshift into Park. Good thing I didn't take Mother's handicap sign, someone's pulling in that space. In that passenger seat, another crinkled-faced snarling lady yells at that driver.

I wriggle my belly out from behind the steering wheel, slam the car door way too hard, and stomp toward Kroger's entrance. As I pass the handicap parking, the man steps from his car, with the old woman still screeching. The man's my age but bigger, wearing a ridiculous sweater of Christmas trees and Elves. His eyes meet mine—pupils spinning—manic. I must look like this.

Reach for a shopping cart in the lobby. I yank and yank and they're stuck and *SHIT!* and yank and it pulls free and I stumble back—"Watch it, Asshole!"—nearly crashing into a mother steering three crying children in a Humvee cart. I mumble something like sorry and push my way into—*what the hell!*—wave at the sensor—*OPEN DAMN IT!*—into the store and slalom my way through the leftovers of humanity to the frozen food aisle.

No matter what I get, it'll be wrong. Ice cream. Vanilla is too normal. Chocolate is too rich. Strawberry super odd. Pistachio is, like, Middle Eastern or Muslim. Neapolitan is almost patriotic but no blue, so screw that. I choose Oreo Chips in Vanilla, Triple Fudge Chocolate Chip, and Cookie Dough Cheese Cake flavors. Dumping the load into my cart I turn and there's that parking lot man with his spinning eyes, standing in front of the frozen pies, holding the glass door open, vibrating with rage. He's ready to kill someone. As I pass, I nod, trying for commiseration. A twitch of his cheek is my reply.

The Little Drummer Boy rum-pa-pum-pums for the millionth time. The fluorescents throb. Sweat tickles down my back. My heart does the three-legged race. *When will this holiday be over?* Reaching the end of the aisle I feel a shift in the something and turn back to look. The entire frozen aisle is empty except for the man by the pies and he SLAMS the glass door. The noise explodes as does the glass, raining tinsel chards down across the polished floor. There is a moment of beautiful stillness from the destruction, and then, the man deflates, shoulders hunching, head bowed, waiting for his comeuppance.

"CLEAN UP ON AISLE SIXTEEN, CLEAN UP ON AISLE SIXTEEN."

The man and I exchange looks, and after a moment, we exchange car keys and addresses. He takes my ice cream and I take his pies. There is a lightness in both of us.

Out to the handicap parking. The old lady in his car criticizes me for taking so long. It feels familiar but doesn't hurt. This will work out fine.

MULBERRY AND ME

When it arrived
it was a stick.
With high hopes,
I did nurture it.

The years have spread us
so I prune
to make us both
a bit more jeune.

It grew askew.
it grew lopsided.
Alas, surprise,
so too, I did.

Would that I'd
accept this tree.
So might I—
also me.

THE KID

IT'S NOT LIKE I'd never done it from behind. That time in my art studio in graduate school was memorable. He was post modern and I was retro—the figurative painting gal. That night was a youthful experiment. Twenty years later, this was quite different.

The foreplay was unexpected. The rubbing of his neck against mine was sweet if you ignored the smell. But it wasn't ignorable. I knew the scent—only this wasn't a scent —it was an odor—more than an odor—an assault. Made my eyes sting. A suffocating attack on my sinuses. Even my throat was scorched breathing him in. The smell was goat cheese to the nth degree.

Ok.

Back up.

Pardon me, that's the wrong expression. Let me set the scene.

Saturday night. And why not? The perfect time for a rendezvous. Was I planning on going out that evening? No. Was I planning on getting lucky alone on the farm? No.

Actually it wasn't Saturday night but in the tail end of Saturday afternoon.

There was a moment in the bath when I pressed low on my soapy belly and wondered what good it was. Lying in the tepid water, thinking three-o'clock-in-the-morning thoughts in the afternoon, that's when I heard them.

You know when coyotes get together under the moon and do their howling? This wasn't that. The sun was still out and the sound was a yipping of happiness as the pack ripped some critter apart. They were on the warpath and that path runs through my 20 acres, so I had a job to do.

With 20 acres and no neighbors, I don't exactly stick to protocol. Rubber boots, a bath robe, and a .22 was my getup. I diligently scoured the fence line and the goat pen and didn't hear another peep of wildness, so stepped back into the kitchen. Setting the .22 on the fridge, I started hot water for tea.

With the back door open.

It was very unexpected and quite endearing at first. He walked right in and I thought it funny, so, *welcome to my kitchen*! As I got out the tea biscuits, he seemed to sense something. He came toward me and I knew. It was absurd. But I knew.

My heart was pounding and—why the hell was my heart pounding? I didn't want it to. Was his pounding? I wanted it to. No, that's not right. I felt ill. He was in front of me, turning his head from side to side as if to see me cubistically. I shuddered and his whole being seemed to do the same. He and I were doing a dance far outside of understanding. Why hadn't I gotten dressed after the bath? Why had I left the back door open? Was I really *this* lonely?

His lips quivered as he leaned toward my face. This was absurd. I had to put a stop to it. Yet, *gosh* his foul breath was animalistic. It tore down into my gut. No. Lower. He grunted and my knees went weak.

Nuzzling against me, his stiff bristles scraped my cheek. I breathed like I wanted him. This was not me. Couldn't be me. Not possibly me.

He turned his head and—How could hair hurt so much?! I wanted to push him away but his deep guttural moan sent my back tipping. Arching.

That must have signaled him for he raised his head, looked at me sideways with a golden eye and rectangular pupil and just as I wondered if he saw in widescreen—he came at me, forehead leading—and the tete-a-tete dropped me to my knees.

The next happened quickly. His teeth on the back of my neck. His hooves pinning my arms. He slid in easily. I'm embarrassed to say, I was ready. Thrust and thrust and thrust and he was off, bellowing two tones simultaneously. Biblical trumpeting resonating through his thick spiraling horns. A shofar.

And there on the dirty linoleum, I watched as Bruno trotted out the back door, crossed the yard, jumped the fence, and joined the others in the goat pen.

It was dusk. Time to lock them in for the night. I put on jeans and a sweatshirt and went out—part of me trepidatious, part of me feeling something dangerously close to prom-night.

Bruno was in the pen with the other goats and the one sheep. I walked up to him slowly and touched his wide forehead. He bent into my hand, but no more than usual. I rubbed his silken ears. Pulled up on his thick curling horns. Nuzzled his face. Nothing happened. So that was it? That wild event forgotten? I wanted some recognition of what we'd experienced. Maybe that's the problem I've always had with sex. I give it more weight than I should. Bruno was over me in a few seconds. He gave a friendly goat-grunt and nudged me. So did the others. They wanted their evening alfalfa.

After I laid out their feed, an emptiness spread over me. I stepped away from the goats to the one dumb sheep. What kind of person was I? How could that have happened? Shame and self-loathing crumpled me. Francine ate as I clutched her thick coat, pressing my face to her smell of lanolin to see if tears would stick to wool.

I went back in as the lonely moon rose and the coyotes began their nightly brutal cacophony.

A month later it was clear something was happening inside me. I was going to have a baby. DAMN!

They always said, "Oh, you'd be such a good mother!" What am I supposed to do with that? Of course I'd be a good mother! I'm kind. I could cuddle the thing.

Cuddle It.

The thing.

The baby.

I was thinking all this. And of course I was thinking of aborting it. But even as I Googled local clinics to get rid of it, I was also looking up the gestation periods of goats. I've always been a curious sort. I needed to see what might emerge, so I stopped looking up abortion clinics. There was only one path for me. This was going to be my baby, or my hell, but my something.

Research online provided little as to when the creature might be born. Would it be the five months of goats or the nine months of humans?

I wondered if I could be called a Nanny or a doe now.

At three months the movement began. Constant punching and kicking. With each kick I'd wonder—is that a little wrinkled foot or a hoof? I'd read that horns didn't start growing until after birth, so I was fairly sure I wasn't about to be gored from inside.

Would it be a Satyr? A human face and torso with a goat's legs and horns? Would it be the opposite? A goat's face and body with a human's legs and ears. That would be weird.

My belly expanded. That was normal, I know. But the other stuff, I didn't know. Like the smell of goat cheese rising from my crotch.

Having heard of about fetal alcohol syndrome and cautious that it might affect goat DNA, I'd not had a drink since. Since what? The attack? Rape? Seduction? Bruno did to me what he'd always done to the does on the farm, so I couldn't judge.

Back to drinking. Not true. I did have a drink. Right afterward. I drank that whole bottle of red that I was saving for guests or a special occasion. I don't have guests and so I figured this was a special occasion. It was the first sex I'd had in several years. More years than I want to count.

Maybe that's why I romanticized it. That's understandable. I hope.

Six months and the ladies in the grocery store were giving me knowing smiles and touching my belly. They backed off quickly when they were kicked in the palm.

I'd taken to greens more than a normal body should. Fiber was not even the word for it. My mouth was constantly grinding on something. Celery. Kale. Stalks of Brussels sprouts. Mastication was what I craved.

Seven months to the day, I bend in pain and—bleat. It's starting. I can't go to a hospital. No one will understand whatever comes out. But I don't want to be alone. I need friends.

It's dark. The field is slippery under my rubber boots. The flashlight shakes as I cross to the pen. Bruno bellows his shofar sound and I imagine that's concern in his eyes as I unlatch the gate. His nose presses my churning kicking whirling swell and he raises his lips to gather the scents and with a hard nudge, pushes me into the dark stall. I collapse on the straw.

Take care of me, Bruno. Widescreen pupils tilt at me. Pain coming often. Bruno's tongue is on my forehead. I'm a salt-lick now.

The moon is full and everyone's gathered over me— Lulu, Danton, Nina, Sierra, Jack, and wooly Francine. All stare with their rectangular eyes, except Francine who has regular eyes. I pull off my panties and a steam of familiarity rises.

What happens next is panting and bleating and blood and rushes of pain and rushes of fluid and I want it to stop but it doesn't and I see in their eyes they have been here before and will be again and we are all doing this and will be and it will go on forever and that is the lesson, except I can't bear a lesson right now because there is no end to the pain and the moon is shaking and all the bleating blends into a single note as something is pushed and the moon is squeezed and there's a massive letting go as it slides free and all those rectangular eyes turn round as the moon shines yellow in each one.

And in the darkness, in that darkness, shaking in the straw, I slow my breathing. I wonder what is this thing that slipped from me. It's clearing its lungs, coughing up its birth between my legs. That quivering thing I can't see—Should it live? Should it be? Should it be loved?

In the darkness of the stall, the others do the licking. They clean the creature and push it towards me through the damp sticky straw. I can't see it but I put a hand down to find a wet mass of slippery energy. It smells my breast and with amazing strength, rams me with its downy forehead and starts suckling.

And in the darkness of the stall, I hear my baby pull in a breath and let out a sound. It's short and fleeting, but clear.

"Maaaa."

SUMMER OF HOPE

IT WAS A SHINY summer day—the kind seen in postcards or old photographs. Sun glittering off the lake. People smiling in bathing suits, waving to the Instamatic. *Wish you were here* and all that.

Darlene saw the scene as if taking the picture. The photograph might be of a family outing. Mother setting up the picnic, sixteen-year-old sister Amanda sunbathing with eyes closed, Father standing proudly, surveying the idyllic view. It might include the fourteen-year-old boy at the end of the dock in his Waxahachie T-shirt, rolled-up jeans, and Indian-bead belt, sunlight haloing his crewcut. The photograph might be taken the moment he was turning, raising a hand in greeting as if to imply something about happiness.

But this wasn't a photograph. The boy was Darlene's jerk brother and his raised hand carried no greeting, only the gesture Mother had smacked him for that morning.

Darlene stuck out her tongue and cursed *Go to HELL!* in her head—secretly happy that the bad word came easily now.

"Lunch is ready," Mother yelled over the cicadas' drone.

As her brother practiced his cowboy stride back from the dock, Darlene wiped a strand of wet hair away from her sunburned cheek, and with a slight smile, let her hand glide off—linger in the air—a secret wave to the imagined camera. Mounted in the photo album, the picture might be cooed over by perfumed aunts after Sunday dinner. Like all the others, it would show no clues of the muggy oppressive air, the things unsaid, or the scabs picked anew, moment to moment.

Darlene's awkward pounds were pressed in the pink hand-me-down bathing suit. She wasn't the same shape as her older sister and her flesh ballooned over the top. The painful buds had grown all during seventh grade last year and no one looked at her face anymore. These days, her father kept jiggling her arms, singing old MacDonald—"Here a moo, there a moo, everywhere a moo-moo."

Now he was standing over Darlene's sunbathing sister, moving his hand in the air as if conducting to the music on the transistor radio. Maybe he was seeing if the dark fingers of his shadow-hand tickled her skin.

A green damselfly landed on Darlene's bare knee and she stifled the urge to shout at the blessing. She was too grownup for that. Besides, girls were supposed to be scared of bugs. Watching it fan its fairy wings, she imagined again, just for old time's sake, that it was Tinker Bell and could grant wishes.

"What is your wish?" Tinker Bell asked.

Darlene ran through the options in her head. Robbie in Math class who smiled at her. Mr. Martin's hand on her shoulder. Only good things. Not any bad things.

Her brother's comic book flattened Tinker Bell.

Darlene kicked him rather than calling out for justice. She was too old for that crybaby stuff and *telling* always made things worse.

"I'm not saying it again," Mother said again. Mother threatened the family with death. She'd slaved over the picnic in the wee hours of the morning while they all got their beauty rest. "People die from mayonnaise. You let it sit any longer, don't say I didn't warn you."

Deviled ham and sliced olives mingled with the probably deadly mayonnaise. Years later Darlene might buy a small can of the pink meat and the enriched bread for nostalgia's sake, only to be gagged by the salty memory. She might feed the sandwich and the spit-out bite to the wagging Labrador or Pekinese she hoped to have someday, when the time was right and she was living on her own, in an apartment in the city, typing for a firm, wearing lipstick, and high heels and hose.

The Wonder Bread stuck to the top of Darlene's retainer, making it pull against her gums painfully. Watered down Bug Juice rinsed off most of the mass. Maybe she would die from the mayonnaise. She would lie in the hospital, everyone gathered around, worried and sad, telling her how much she would be missed. She would be able to say everything she never could because it was the end. "Tell Mr. Martin I liked his class. Tell Robbie in Math his smile always made me happy." Everyone would cry that such a kind heart as hers—beat no more.

Darlene's older sister lowered the straps of her bathing suit and rolled onto her stomach, turning up the transistor for *Listen, Do You Want to Hear a Secret?* The Fab Four. Would this be the closest that Romance got to Darlene? Flipping through their bubble-gum cards? Imagining? Or would there be a man in a suit at the firm? Up in the skyscraper. Maybe he'd look like Mr. Martin and smoke a pipe that smelled like Christmas and cookies and not sticky tobacco fingers.

Darlene's father flicked the ash from his Lucky Strike and pulled in the smoke. She watched the bull's breath stream from his nose. He turned to her, winking—and she crossed her freckled arms to cradle her jaded thirteen-year-old heart.

Romance wasn't around the corner for her. Not this summer. Maybe not ever.

Wasn't it just last week that her best friend Julie had slipped her a folded note, listing the ten reasons no one liked her? Maybe Julie was only teasing. *Just kidding,* they always said. *Can't you take a joke?* Darlene needed to learn how to take a joke. How not to let things hurt.

But still, there was cause for hope. She'd gotten the wishes in before Tinker Bell had been squashed. School was only two weeks away and she'd have Mr. Martin and Robbie and maybe some new faces in class. There was lots to look forward to. Soon the weather would cool. Leaves would dance across the sidewalk on Halloween.

And in November, President Kennedy was coming to Dallas.

YOU ARE CHINESE WATER TORTURE

What drives me crazy is not the
constant dripping—
But the
waiting
between
drops.

The anticipation
and tension
as I look
skyward
for the
next
slow
splash.

Would that my Chinese torturer
would feel pity on me
and twist
the faucet
just a bit
to let a

thin
steady
stream
of you
trickle
down
my
face.

OLD DOG, NEW TRICKS

"IF I'D KNOWN how you kids'd turn out I wouldn't have bothered." Her milky eyes blink at me.

Stop. Look away. Breathe. Almost done.

Outside, the snow continues. Something to stare at other than her.

"What was I saying, Davie?" She sputters and a flick of something lands on my hand.

She's got me confused with my brother again. I could pretend I *am* Davie and ask her about Philip. I could find out what she really thinks of me.

Bad idea.

I pull up a smile. "I'm Philip."

There's a flash of rage in her eyes. "Don't try to trick me!"

She's a feeble 92 to my 65, but her look still shrinks me.

The grandfather clock chimes. Another fifteen minutes gone.

Nurse Sharlyne comes in with her round brown face, bringing relief from white walls, white plastic chairs, and pale transparent skin.

Sharlyne talks loud so the old ears can hear. "You doin' fine, Miss Clark? Every thing good, Miss Perris?"

How she can tell them apart? They all look alike. Colorless hair. Stooped shoulders. Vacant blinking eyes.

Sharlyne smiles at me, "Got plans for the weekend?"

"I'm too old for plans." I say, hoping to sound funny.

"Nobody's too old for plans, Mr. Philip—"

"This is my son *Davie*," Mother interrupts.

Sharlyne bends close to Mother, "Miss Jessup, this son's been coming every day, visitin' you since long before I came here. This son is Philip. Far as I seen, Davie ain't no count."

"You don't know," Mother snarls.

"I know what I know. You need anything, Mr. Philip?"

I mouth *thank you* while shaking my head *no*, which turns out harder than I expected. Sharlyne's brown eye winks as she moves past.

Mother's mouth opens and her tongue searches the yellow teeth for words. "She doesn't know my sons. Philip's the boy married that Janice woman."

"*Janet* not *Janice*." Thirty-two years of marriage and she still can't get my wife's name right.

"What was I saying, Davie?"

Why does she think I'm Davie? He's short like Dad was. Never visits. Bet she wouldn't even recognize him if he walked in now. But he won't. He's off having fun in sunny Phoenix. No winter in Phoenix.

The snow is really coming down. It'll be a rough drive home.

"Davie!"

"I'm *Phil-ip!*"

"Don't you yell at me!" Mother spits.

Best to be silent now. Outside, the patio fountain is wrapped against the cold. Mummified. When will this winter end? Be patient. Soon.

I look to the right of Mother's ear, at the fish-bowl on the counter filled with little bright pieces. What are those pieces of color in this monotone room?

My boots have salt stains from the snow. By my dirty boot there's a piece of a jigsaw puzzle. This could be the piece everyone's been looking for. I bend to pick it up and my pants tighten round the waist. I should diet, but I know that's long past happening.

The puzzle piece has a tip of green. Shrub or a tree. A yellow edge of a building, a window? A touch of red. Flower box? Gardenias? Maybe this was from a village scene. A colorful village somewhere nice. Costa Rica maybe.

Out the window the snow swirls. It'll be dark when I get home. Janet never puts the porch light on. What is her class tonight? Sewing? She'll leave the usual note. *Back at ten. Heart shape. J.* I always tell her she should use the same piece of paper and save on trees. She always says she will but that would make her a "tree hugger" type.

That girl the final year at Syracuse, before I stopped painting—what was her name?—she was a tree-hugger type. From Costa Rica. I had just enough Spanish to her English. That hiking trip we took, two of us in one sleeping bag. Skin so smooth. What was her name? Celestina? Would she have left the same note every night? Would she go to classes and return after I'm in bed? Would she have made me different?

Grandfather chimes again. Another 15 minutes gone. Sharlyne moves through the room. I wave her over, "Found this piece of puzzle. Someone might be missing it."

Sharlyne tosses it in the fish-bowl behind Mother. "These are *all* missing pieces. Pieces that don't belong nowhere. Sometimes someone dumps this bowl out and tries to make sense of it, thinking it's one big puzzle. Lord, do they have a time!" She laughs and squeaks her white shoes out to the hall.

Hundreds of lost pieces with no place to go. They'll never find the place they belong. Oh, stop.

It's getting dark. Winter's early-dark. Roads will be dangerous. I'll stay 'til the next chimes, then make my good-byes.

A black crow lands on the handicap railing outside, perched in the frozen white wasteland, a winter landscape. The bird looks like it's waiting for something. A death? Maybe there'll be one soon. Maybe before the snow melts.

Mother's a winter landscape, too. Hair white. Skin white. Eyes pale, but her pupils are black. Black crows in the snow.

I make the effort and wrestle up another smile. It's like most of my clothes these days: tight and barely covering what it should. "Snow coming down hard. Remember how Dad loved the snow? He'd tinker with the blower like it was a race car and—"

"Dullard. That man was nothing. My life was wasted with dullards."

The crows in her eyes glare at me. She's including me, no doubt.

"Dad was a good provider. He put up with a lot." I shouldn't have said that. She'll know I mean her.

"*I* put up with a lot. I could have had *anyone*. I had— *pizazz!*"

There's no use saying more. Her dander is up and won't be coming down. Where is that clock chime? Where is Sharlyne?

Snow scatters against the window, pixelating the view like a TV screen on the blink.

Her chuckling sounds like choking. There's a twinkle in her eye, "Snowing hard. Like that time at the boat house."

"Boat house?"

"Snowed in all night. Couldn't get to us if they'da tried. Lucky me. Don't tell—" Mother looks at the other old women as if they have their hearing aids turned to *Maximum*. Splotches of red dot her winter cheeks as she whispers, "We did more than neck."

This is new. "Who?"

"Gosh, he was swell. You look just like him." The crows in her eyes dance. "There for the winter semester. We did everything under the sun. He was kicked out for being a hooligan. I had pizazz. He saw it. Shoulda married him 'stead of the other."

A jolt of something hits my stomach. "The other? You mean Dad?"

"By the time I knew, Orville was gone and it wasn't a time you could up and have a baby alone, so I took the dullard's offer."

The florescent tubes shine bright, humming loudly. "Dad wasn't my father?"

"Orville was your father. Orville."

The room's tilting. I never looked like Dad. Davie looks like Dad. But Mother gets things jumbled.

I try to sound casual. "Orville. What was his last name?"

Mother's eyes travel over me like I'm him. "You loved the hooch. Made you wild and sometimes mean. But lord, we had a time, didn't we?"

She's never looked at me like this. The judgment leaves her face. Her wrinkles fade and the girl from the old photograph slyly winks at me.

The blood rushes to my face. I don't want to see this side of her. But I have to know. Breathing in quick, I smile in a way I don't ever smile. "Marge, we were quite a pair." I take her hand and hold it in a way I don't ever hold it. "You could have been Mrs. Orville—"

Mother's eyes are dreamy. "Mrs. Orville—"

"What was my last name, Marge?"

The clock chimes and Sharlyne comes in.

Mother'll lose this thread any moment. I grin at the nurse, "I'm Orville. We're trying to remember my last name."

Sharlyne tucks the blanket close around Mother. "Don't mind your son, Miss Jessup, he jes playin' with you."

"My son?—"

"I'm Orville. My last name—"

Mother's expression turns familiar. "Why are you badgering me?! I'm tired!"

Sharlyne smiles at me, as if apologizing for a naughty child. "Best let your mama rest."

"I'm sorry, Mother. The man, Orville, he's my father?"

Sharlyne tilts her head. *Father?* she mouths at me.

The black crows in Mother's eyes nod in unison as she sings, "Father, bother, mother, smother, shutter, butter."

She's gone now. Off in fragments.

I stare at the fish-bowl of lost puzzle pieces. I'm left with a missing piece that might be a father.

My winter dusk envelops me. Snow covers everything and she may be gone before it melts.

Mother lowers her parchment eyelids over the bowing crows.

My hearing aid squeals as Philip kisses my cheek. He's sweating. I want to wipe my face but I don't, so he'll think I'm sleeping. I hear him pull on his heavy winter coat and pause, waiting for more, but I'm done.

"See you tomorrow, Mother," he whispers and when he finally lumbers out, I open my eyes.

That boy has gotten old. *Some* might say it's "tendin' to his mama" but I know better. He got old the day he married that Janet woman. She sucked the life out of him.

"You want me to take you back t'your room now, Miss Jessup?" Nurse asks. "You a mite tired now."

"Not tired, bored."

This makes her laugh. "What you bored about? You had a nice visit with your son 'til you got mixed up."

I try not to grin but feel my lips twitching.

"You trying to be Mona Lisa with that smile, Miss Jessup?"

"Just entertaining myself."

Nurse shakes her head. "You need to spread a little kindness on that man. He's all you got and he may get sick of you."

"Bother someone else," I hiss, and try to spit at her, but it only lands on my cracked lip.

"Why you so mean?" Nurse asks quietly. "You steal playin' cards from the decks and puzzle pieces too. You hide people's glasses. You a mean old lady. Some day your son may see you clear and never come back."

"He'll come back. Especially now. Needs to find out about Orville."

"Who's this Orville? Your son said he was his father—"

I can't hide my grin. "There isn't any Orville. I made him up. I was bored."

Nurse jerks back like I'm a rattlesnake. Triumph spreads up my chest as she hurries away.

In the big window, the darkness outside has been replaced by this white room. In the center there's an old lady slumped in a wheelchair. She doesn't look like me, but she wipes the spittle round her mouth when I wipe mine.

Snow swirls in the headlights, accelerating and zooming past like I'm traveling through outer space. Wipers screech and thwap, screech and thwap. The defroster doesn't seem to be working. The windshield is fogging. Or is that my eyes?

Could I be another man's son? Philip, son of Orville. She said he was—what was it?—a hooligan. Could I be the son of a hooligan? A tincture of pride warms my face. What do you get to do if you're a hooligan? Could I manage? Probably not. The glow cools to shame. Turn on the radio to drown it out.

The road is slick with wet snow, already needs more plowing. Flares burn up ahead, haloed red in the whirling flakes. I press the breaks lightly to slow without losing control.

Past the flaming warnings, rear flashers blink on the left, a car belly-up in the snow. Hope no one's hurt. Or worse. Several cars have pulled over and silhouetted figures move about, so I'm not needed. Good thing. Wouldn't know what to do.

Past the wreck, I speed up a touch.

Mother and Orville. Why didn't Dad ever say anything?

Public Radio reminds me to subscribe but Janet already gave. Someone will win a trip for two to Bermuda. Hope it isn't us. Janet's not one for the beach and drinks with umbrellas *"on principle."* Besides, I can't wear a bathing suit. Those days are over.

I change the station to oldies.

The driveway's got six inches already. Better shovel before Janet gets home.

Gear slides into park when that song starts. I turn off the motor but leave the headlights and radio on.

That song. Celestina loved this band. We picked unripe walnuts and made a liqueur. Noir something. She was always laughing. *Querido*, she called me.

When the song ends, I lumber out and start shoveling. It's hard work but I make progress with every stab of the blade into snow.

Mission accomplished, I head inside and passing through the vestibule, I turn on the porch light. Janet doesn't like me wasting energy, but I think it's cozier to come home to some light.

The kitchen's dark but for the blue microwave clock. Table's empty but for the mail. Janet's note is usually front and center. Nothing tonight. Maybe she didn't go out. Maybe she's still here. Maybe she's taking a nap. Maybe she slipped in the shower.

"Janet?"

The house whistles where I didn't mount that storm window right.

I check the bathroom and bedroom. No one. But I've tracked snow all over. I'll hear about that.

Maybe Janet decided the note was redundant. Or maybe there was an emergency. There was a call and she raced off. A death? Mother died and Janet was racing out to meet me. The roads were slippery and she was driving fast. Maybe it was her car belly-up flashing red by the side of the road. Mother is dead and Janet is dead.

A flush of something cascades through me, tumbling my heart, making it lurch against my parka. The empty house feels open and infinite. If it were true—the dim light from the microwave clock, the refrigerator's buzz, the endless winter—could disappear. Replaced with—could it have happened?—replaced with— something new?

Maybe her note's under the mail.

Bill from AT&T. AARP renewal. Christmas card, return address: Phoenix. Got to be Davie and Susan.

I skim their yearly update. Trips, golf tournaments, news of the super-achieving kids. There's a picture of a fat, bug-eyed baby. Grandchild number one.

The ice melting from my sleeve drips onto the photo raising a glossy pimple on the baby's cheek. I move my arm, dripping more, creating leprous flesh all over the face.

What if the wreck was Janet? Should I call her cell phone? If she's alive she'll be angry that I'm interrupting her class and she'll remind me we pay by the minute. If she was in the accident, I'll know before too long. Someone will knock on the door, hat in hand. Good thing I shoveled the drive.

Nurse bends close as she lifts my feet and places them on the tile floor.

"This floor is too cold!" I yell. "Bring me a mat."

A grunt is her response as she locks the wheels.

"You can be silent forever for all I care," I say, lifting my arm.

Nurse slides her big soft shoulder under mine and with a twirl she has me up and spinning and raising my nightgown just enough as she sets me down on the toilet seat. Usually she says something funny right about now. Tonight she's got a monument face on.

"Git! I'll call when I'm done."

Nurse leans close. "I'd as soon leave you settin' here all night, 'cept I'm a good person."

She slides out the door. Ha! I got her talking!

This seat hurts my bones. The lights are too bright. I can't remember how to pee. I try to let go. Push.

I *did* have pizazz.

I don't remember where I waited. Maybe behind a tree. I remember watching the boys laughing and shoving as they left the boathouse and started their slog through the snow. Orville wasn't with them so I slipped inside. The boathouse was cold. Orville must have had to store the equipment as punishment for something he'd done. He was cursing low with his movie star lips. He saw me and said, "Scram," but I didn't. I knew if he saw I was willing, he'd want me. We could stay in the boathouse all night. Tell people we were snowed in. He kept cursing and putting things away. I lay back on the tarps, trembling. Ready. He ignored me. When he finished the chores, he went to the door and gestured for me to get up. I pretended to twist my ankle and asked him to walk me to my dorm. He didn't want to be seen with me. Told me to turn out the lights and left me there. Only time we ever talked.

Tinkling sound in the bowl but I feel water from my eyes. Water spilling over the cheeks I lost years ago. Trickling down my neck, getting caught in the maze of wrinkles.

Why is a full-length mirror facing the toilet? What idiot thought this up? The hag grimaces at me, tears glistening on her withered face. I raise my hand to show her what I think of her and she lifts her claw, middle finger crooked high.

Go to hell.

Nurse should have knocked by now. She's punishing me.

I don't care. I don't need her. I can get in that damn chair myself.

Grab both armrests. Push and push and pull and unstick from the bowl, dragging forward, leaning, leaning. Can't go back, can't go forward. "NURSE!" Damn her! "NURSE!"

I can't hold this. I'll die like all the old—falling. The withered witch in the mirror looks horrified, glaring at me from her worthless carcass, arms shaking like feeble stalks powered by sagging rubber-bands. I hate her so much I almost hope her arms give out. "NURSE!" the ghoul in the mirror screams.

White uniform blots out the hag and lifts and I'm turned and wet hits cold on the back of my legs as Nurse clicks her tongue. "Lordy, what am I gonna do with you? You got your nighty soaked."

In bed. Wondering. Is Janet dead? What if—

Everything is easy on the internet these days. Airline tickets. Hotels. Researching local customs. Do I still have a suitcase? When was the last time I used one? Before they all had wheels that's for sure.

Headlights roll across the ceiling pulling me from my thinking. Or was it planning?

Headlights go out. Is it Janet or a police cruiser? Car door shuts. Wait. Listen for a knock. Sounds of keys. Janet's home. Porch light off. Purse down.

Things are as they were. Are as they will always be. Breathe out *what if*. Breathe in *what is*. Light goes on in the bathroom. Should I pretend I'm asleep? If we don't talk tonight, we won't see each other until tomorrow night when I'm back from Mother and she's back from her thing. Tomorrow's Thursday. Is that sandwiches for the homeless?

Bathroom light off. She slides into bed.

I lie still. I should tell her about Orville. What would she think if I wasn't the man she thought I was? Would she see me in a new way?

I slide my hand over to find her shoulder.

"Oo. Cold."

"Sorry." I should touch her with the one that's warm under the covers, but I don't. "Your class thing go okay?"

"It's not a class, it's a meetup."

"You didn't leave a note."

"There's not much point, is there?"

"No."

"You left the porch light on. Our electricity bill was high last month. Can you at least try to remember?"

"I will."

"You won't. I know you. You never change."

I grunt and turn to the window. She knows me. But what if I'm not that man she thinks she knows. Snow whispers against the glass. What if it's warm in Costa Rica.

"You're late," Mother scolds.

"Snow made a mess of route 38. Had to take Collins Road."

"You think I care about roads, Philip?"

At least she knows who I am today. Hopefully she'll remember more about Orville.

Sharlyne's looking at me with her brows pulled down. Did I do something wrong? Snow fell off my boots in the lobby. "Sharlyne, I'm sorry about the snow on the floor."

She shakes her head to show she doesn't care about that. "Mr. Philip, can I have a little a chat with you?"

I *did* do something wrong.

Mother grabs my wrist before I can stand. "Philip and I are chatting. He's visiting *me*, Nurse."

Sharlyne nods. "Afore you leave today." She takes a step back, but hovers nearby.

Got to learn more about Orville, while Mother's fresh. "You mentioned Orville. You said he was my real father. I—"

"You want a sweet, Miss Jessup?" Sharlyne interrupts, unwrapping a peppermint.

Mother holds out her palm and Sharlyne gives her the candy.

"The boathouse, Mother. Orville?"

"Don't get Miss Jessup talkin' or she'll choke on the sweet."

Sharlyne steps away. Mother's lips pucker, as she rolls the candy around. Her jaw drops and rises, drops and rises, sinking hollows in her pale cheeks like she's nursing on an unseen breast. I can't watch.

Outside, a bright blue bird lands on the canvas-wrapped fountain. An Indigo Bunting. What are you doing here, bird? Are you lost? Fly south.

Janet dragged me bird watching when we first got married. Tested me on the names. Indigo Bunting. Eastern Phoebe. Yellow-rumped Warbler. Had me carry the guides and gear but finally dismissed me because I made too much noise.

"Stop daydreaming," Mother says, candy clattering.

I pretend she's being nice. Smile. "Wonder where I got that. Maybe Orville? Was he a dreamer?"

Mother bobbles her head. "I don't want to talk about that. I'm bored. Tell me about your wife. What's Janice up to?"

"*Janet! Not Janice! Janet!* It's been thirty-two years and it *was* Janet, *still is* Janet, and *always will be* Janet. What's *Janet* up to? Well, we don't talk. And now, seems we don't even leave notes anymore. She got classes. Meetups. Gardening, social justice something. She's got that and I've got—you. *You're* bored? Join the club."

Step to the window. The lost Indigo Bunting startles and flies away over bare tree-tops. *Not that way! Go South!* I press my fist against the cold glass and pretend I'm contemplating the weather. Sky's darkening. Mother's reflection is fidgeting. Shouldn't have dumped my life onto hers.

He's pretending to look at the weather. Any minute he'll turn around and do that meek smile and apologize. He disgusts me, but I made him.

Be different. Don't be that damaged boy. A tightness in my throat as—there it is—the turn. The meek smile.

"Mother—"

"Don't be a pussy," I blurt out.

Have I ever use that word before? Maybe it's true what they say about getting older, or have I always been this way?

As he looks away my son's back doesn't tell me much, but his shoulders are hunched and by his elbow movement I can see he's wiping his face. Crying? Can I still make the boy cry?

Nurse said Philip would disappear-never-to-return if I kept at him.

I try to sound cozy. "Can't expect me to change now. Leopard and its spots. Old dog with new tricks and all that."

His other elbow moves. Lifting his watch. I'm losing him. I'll keep him. I can do it.

"Did I tell you? Orville had a mustache."

His ear cocks toward me.

"A big brassy one. Looked like black wings of a bat. People stared and he liked that."

Philip turns, hooked.

In the window reflection Nurse moves behind my chair. She's spying, wary of me and protective of my boy. She'll give me another candy if I don't watch out. I backtrack, floundering, "Janet, not Janice. I remember. You married her."

Nurse's reflection steps into the hall.

I wave Philip close. "Orville was wild and carefree and reckless. Wasn't one to settle down. Wasn't one for paying bills or buying groceries. He had *balls*!"

"Maybe, but he got you pregnant and walked away—"

"You don't know anything!" I hiss, hoping it's quiet enough that Nurse won't come back. "You *couldn't* know. You're not like him. You turned out like the dullard."

Philip's face tightens.

Why do I do this? Because he's so easy to break?

Philip pulls in a breath and holds it. "Maybe I should take after Orville," he says in a low exhale. "Maybe I should walk away."

"I didn't mean you, Philip. You're a good boy."

"Maybe I shouldn't be a good boy."

This has gone too far. I need to give him a morsel. Give him something to cling to.

What was it Philip liked—golf?—no, that's Davie. Philip liked—come on, brain—Ahh! Painting. "Orville was a painter. Big, brash, expressionist stuff."

A light sparks in Philip's face. Or something. A flash of pride? Philip lets the words out slow, "I used to paint. Remember?"

I've got him now. "You got that from Orville. You should grow a mustache. And paint. Orville would have wanted it —"

Nurse presses her hot hand on my shoulder. "Miss Jessup, you gettin' tired and awful mixed up."

"STAY OUT OF THIS OR I'LL SEE YOU FIRED!" I scream.

Nurse snaps upright. The old ladies in the room stare at me.

Philip shakes his head. "You can't fire Sharlyne, Mother. She doesn't work for you. If anything, she works for me. I'm paying her. And she's staying."

I don't want this game anymore. "Nurse is right. I'm tired. Come back tomorrow."

Nurse chimes in, "Your mother got plenty tired these last few times. You best cut back on your visits, Mr. Philip."

My son's world grows wide. His eyes dart with the possibilities.

"Once a week?" Philip suggests.

I open my mouth to protest but Nurse barrels through, "Once a month."

Once a month?!

With the thought of it, my son gets lighter and straighter. At sixty-something he looks like a man for the first time.

His face is circling me, waiting for permission.

He thinks I'll say no.

He thinks I can't manage without him.

He thinks I need him.

I'll show him.

"Once a month," I make my voice say.

Nurse lets out a sigh and her shoes squeak away.

Philip's glowing. He's glad to be rid of me. He needs to remember his place. I'll tell him something more. Something about Orville. He—died penniless. Died in jail. Was alone and homeless. Died of the clap.

"Another thing about Orville—" I whisper to my son.

The squeaking stops.

Nurse returns and I feel her heat behind me. Philip smiles at her, a twinkle in his eye. "Sharlyne, Mother's been telling me about Orville. Orville's my real dad."

She'll tell my son that I made Orville up and Philip'll leave forever. I twist to look up at her. I put *please* in my eyes. Revenge flits over her face as she turns back to my boy.

"This Orville be what I wanted to talk on, Mr. Philip," Nurse says calmly.

Philip grins at Nurse. "Did you know I used to paint? Since I've got a month, my plan is to start painting again. Make a new start. Seems Orville was quite the painter."

"I heard," Nurse says. "Miss Jessup tol' me all about him."

Everything in me slumps. She'll get the truth out and I'll lose my son.

Nurse shakes her head. "Quite a man, Mr. Orville. I'm *glad* you got told 'bout your real father. Never too late to change and be someone else."

My old heart flutters as Philip blooms with a radiant smile.

Nurse laughs and flicks her hand to shoo him. "Best let your mama rest."

Philip stands, flipping on his coat. "Gonna cultivate a little of the old man. See what it's like to run off and leave the bills and groceries to someone else." He brushes his lips against my cheek, looking close into my eyes. "And next time, next month, I'll be sporting a mustache and a tan. Gonna leave winter and head somewhere warm to paint. Always had a hankering to see Costa Rica. I've Orville to thank. And you."

In the window, the reflection of the old lady reaches out a claw-like hand to the man. He holds it with both of his. In the reflection, they look like they could be loving people. From this distance, it seems possible. The man waves and steps away as the view blurs.

Nurse doesn't know what to say. Guess I don't either. She steps off to others but keeps looking back. My eyes won't stop leaking. There's a sad hole inside but it feels warm instead of cold. Maybe it's not a hole, maybe it's an ache from using muscles that never get used.

The clock chimes and Nurse moves next to me. "You doing okay, Miss Jessup?"

"Why didn't you tell my son the truth?" I ask.

"I was set to." Nurse pauses, like she's trying to figure out why herself. "But then—I mean, he got talkin' 'bout the plan to paint. Ain't never heard Mr. Philip with a plan before. Weren't about to stop that." She clicks the brakes off my chair.

"Month's a long time, Sharlyne."

She's surprised I know her name. It makes her glow.

"Yes it is, Miss Jessup. But we can entertain each other. We got this big ol' bowl of puzzle pieces. We can dump it out and see if we can't get some back where they belong."

"That'll take all winter."

"You up to it. You stole most all of them, so that should help." She laughs that cuddling one and turns away.

As she looks out at the falling snow, Sharlyne puts her dark warm hand on mine and it feels good.

LIFE LESSON #346,029

Tonight he cut the cheese
on the bias.

Haphazard
Improvisational
He cut the orange block akimbo.
Big, little, fat, thin,—sideways.

I always cut with straight rules.
T-square
and 90 degree angles.

Tonight I'm confronted by a piece of sharp cheddar
formed from an alternative universe than mine.

It is a whack-up-side-the-head.

There's more than one way to slice a cheese.

TOWEL SOLICE

POP AND I SPEND the morning planing the planks smooth. Not easy with home-hewn wood. He chose the tall pine not because it's the prettiest or oldest but because The Big Oak provides great shade for the porch, the birch is—birch, and the pecan gives us all a reason to live with Mom's pies. So pine it is. Years on the logging teams has him knowing exactly where to cut, how to adjust the back-cut so it falls just so. He makes it crash precisely by the barn so it's near the tools. The chainsaw roars and then the band saw and now father and son are in a steady rhythm of *swish, swish, swish* with our planes.

The length should be obvious but Pop wants leg room so we add six inches. *Swish. Swish.* My brow drips onto the fresh wood. He won't let us use the electric sander. Wants sweat mixed with the sap. I'm happy to sweat—*I want what he wants.*

Mom calls from the kitchen and we head in for lunch but she stops us at the door. "Hose down. You're covered with sawdust."

We do as ordered and what should be perfunctory self hosing becomes a water fight. Pop uses the dog bowl as weapon, then shield. Seeing their property absconded with Artimus and Zelda bark and snap at the flying spray. I use the hose to keep Pop at bay but he is a trickster and chops the hose with the woodpile ax and commandeers the short weaponized end. I'm soaked.

Three bongs of the dinner-bell-porchlight-hood send us turning off the water and shaking like the happy dogs. Mom tosses us both large blue bath towels and we dry off, leaving them in wet lumps on the porch steps.

In the kitchen, Mom serves us grilled cheese on her homemade bread with garden-tomato soup. She gestures out the sink window. "So I can see from there. Not to close, but close enough."

Pop nods, dunking his burnt bread edge into the red liquid. "I'll get out there after, you give me a spot, and I'll drop a stake."

I have trouble swallowing my sandwich despite dunking it in the soup. *Don't think. Keep focused on the projects at hand.*

After our refueling, Pop heads out toward the tall grass by cow pasture with a five pound hammer and wooden stake. He watches the kitchen window. Mom points left. Pop steps until she holds up her hand. She gestures forward and he walks one step, two, three- *Stop!* Mom wanders about in the kitchen a bit, pretending to prep food and whatnot while glancing out at Pop. She has him take another two steps to the right and gives her thumbs up. Pop pounds in the stake.

The afternoon is spent with more planing, then measuring, cutting, and dovetailing the angled joints. We finish a little before sunset. It's simple and sturdy but with touch of elegance. "Just like me," Pop says, knocking on the lid and turning away to indicate we're done. We step out of the barn into the world swirling with life. Grasshoppers, dragon flies, bees, and sparrows, all backlit with the setting sun's glow. Pop's white hair joins in. He punches my arm, grabs a shovel, and leads me toward the stake in the tall grass by Lulu and Elmer's pasture.

Pop pulls the stake from the ground and stands in its spot. He takes in the view, rotating slowly. "Garden. Pond. Cows. Mountain. Forest. Home. Sky." He hands me the shovel. "You ever see the movie Cool Hand Luke?"

"You know I have."

"So you know what to do. I'm gonna take a lie down."

He heads back inside and I start digging.

The rich ground is moist and easy to dig. It's the Pacific Northwest, so of course we've had rains. It's okay goin' for the first three feet. I keep working and those rains suddenly appear. Earth turns to mud and mud to slurry and a squishing makes me turn. Pop in his yellow mac and tall boots backlit by the porch light. "Come on in, son. Ain't nothing that can't wait 'nother day."

As we start toward the house, Pop stops. "You hear that?"

I listen. "No."

"You sure?" he asks. "Listen."

I try again. The rain patters off the tall trees causing splashes around us. A call of a bird—a loon? Pop would know, but I don't ask. I shake my head in answer.

"Come—over by the laundry line."

I follow Pop doing a kind of cartoon sneaky tip-toeing. By the soaking clothes he taps his ear. "Hear?"

He moves along the dripping items. Jeans, dish cloths, underwear, work shirts—"Listen."

The large blue towel, black in the darkness, drips, pulling heavily at the line.

"Hear it? It's sayin', 'Hey, Pappy, you gonna leave me out all night?'" Pop leans close to the hanging towel. "No, I am gonna take you in to get cozy and warm and you're gonna be ready for another beautiful day very soon!"

He pulls off the clothes-pins and drapes the towel over his arm. "Let's get you inside, kiddo."

I follow. Pop is always playing but this feels different.

Inside, Pop drapes the towel across the back of a chair and pushes it close to the smoldering fireplace. "You'll be fine now. Rest and have no worries," he says, patting the cloth. Then he turns to me. "Thanks for the digging. I'll help with it tomorrow."

And we all go to bed. I fall asleep picturing the towel basking in the fire's warmth.

Morning brings biscuits and sausage gravy even though that's not on anyone's diet. Ginger preserves and raspberries from the yard. Pop pulls the blue towel from the chair by the fireplace. It's crunchy from the heat. He drapes it around his shoulders and walks out of the house like a king. Mom and I exchange a glance but know not to linger. She smiles and turns to wash the dishes as I head out.

The digging goes well. I dig and Pop supervises. When I take a break, Pop and I throw clods of dirt at each other. We do "mud angels" in the muck. We'll certainly have to use that severed hose again before going inside!

Pop mops his body with the towel and wraps it turban-like around his head. "What? What are you saying?" He cocks his head as if listening and turns to me. "Towel's worried about you."

I feel a loosening at my knees—*Keep it together!* I breathe in. "Tell towel I'm gonna take care of everything. Towel has nothing to worry about."

Pop nods and spears his shovel into the large dirt mound beside the deep rectangular pit. "Let's have a picnic."

And we do. It's leftover biscuits and more berries and ice cream and Spam we didn't know we had and baked beans and the dogs dance around knowing they'll get all the leftovers and the shadows move from one side of the world to the other and the insects are backlit again and there's wine now and a second picnic of peaches and Lulu and Elmer's butter on Mom's bread and the record player is brought out with The Big Extension Cord and we dance to the Talking Heads and Tom Waits and John Prine and Billie Holiday and Hoagy Carmichael and Pop rolls Towel into a tube and lies back with it under his head to look at the stars wink and shimmy. And the grave is already dug and the casket already built and now, as I look at Pop on the grass, silent and still, I know when it comes time to move him, I'll drape Towel over his body and repeat over and over to that cloth, "Everything's gonna to be alright."

INTO THE SILENT NIGHT

THREE DAYS before Christmas and the forecast was for snow. First large storm of the season. I was okay with it as long as I got to walk home before it started. Being socked in for the holiday didn't bother me. I'd buy bourbon and cold-cuts and be fine.

It was ten to five and already dark. In the Wire Room, teletype machines were rat-a-tatting from the Associated Press, Reuters, and United Press International, but here in the City Room, the phones' insistence was diminishing and winter coats were being wrestled with. I stubbed out my cigarette, turned off the humming Selectric typewriter, and stood to leave.

My telephone rang. Friday night on December 23rd was not a time to die. I ignored it. Five rings later I answered, "Obits. Jack Curtis here."

"Rob at East General. Got one."

"You have no heart," I said retrieving the Bic from behind my ear. "Ready."

"Stanley Freeman. Age 62. Found at the bus stop outside Town Topic Hamburgers. They called it in. He worked there."

"Wallet?"

"License. Six bucks. Expired library card. No pictures, no emergency contacts."

I wished Rob happy holidays and hung up. If I hurried I could get this written, to the copy room, and be out by five. I called Town Topic.

"Stanley's been flipping burgers since way back. He came sometime after the war. Like '48 or something. He was a fixture."

"Worked there thirty-five years? What do you know about him?"

The co-workers conferred: Friendly but never talked much. Family unknown. Didn't socialize.

I hung up and searched for Stanley in the white pages. Lived at the Midwest Arms. Gave the manager a call. He was happy for the news. "Man's been in the room for forever. Now I can raise the rent."

To my questions: "He paid on time. Cash. Quiet. No next of kin on file."

I stared at the City Room. The television showed Reagan saying something to cheer us for the season. A few typewriters still clattered but most folks had left to avoid the storm and start the holiday. Heading for home and hearth. Family and friends.

I turned my Selectric on and typed the words: *Stanley Freeman. 62 years. Burger flipper at Town Topic Hamburgers.*

Not even half an inch of copy.

Switched off the hum. Grabbing my coat and scarf I stripped the page from the typewriter and carried it across the wide room. Time to turn in the obit and leave. Only, I couldn't.

Bert was still in his office as I knew he would be. Forever the stalwart reporter at The Star. Plus he had no one waiting at home. Like me.

"Have a sec?" I asked.

Bert put out his hand and I gave him the copy. Quick read.

"Shit," he said.

"Yeah."

"Drink?"

I tied my scarf, he hauled on his winter coat, and we stepped downstairs to push into the night.

The cold air stung. My nose hairs crisped. Snowflakes teased, pretending they were the main attraction. We knew better. The real show was on the way.

"Bah humbug," Bert grumbled, his head down to brave the ten steps to Casey's.

Into orange warmth, Jingling Bells, cigarette smoke, and twinkle lights. Captain slid the drinks across the bar's slick counter and we took up residence in our booth. Lifting glasses we toasted *happy holidays*. The first two drinks we told tales of snowy disasters and complained of the commercialization of Christmas as the storm outside intensified. Third brought us back to Stanley Freeman.

Bert grumbled, "A life reduced to a few words. No memorial. No one caring."

Bert was twenty years my senior. Missed all the wars. Had no kids. Divorced years ago. *Bert Rollins. Reporter for the Kansas City Star. No survivors.*

And me? *Jack Curtis. Reporter for the Kansas City Star. No survivors.*

Draining his whiskey, Bert shook his head. "Stanley Freeman. The guy's got to have done *something* interesting."

"No one to ask. He could have played sax with Charlie Parker and we wouldn't know."

"He could have played with Charlie in Paris."

"And danced with Josephine Baker."

"The guy was sixty two. Probably was in the war. Maybe a paratrooper dropping behind enemy lines on D-day—"

"—saved an entire French family from slaughter."

"Marched in victory with the troops along the Champs-Élysées, the Mademoiselles blowing kisses."

We laughed and signaled for another round. Snow battered the window. Holiday music droned. The twinkle lights blurred.

I had an idea. "We could—"

Bert looked at me, his eyes moist. "No one would be the wiser," he said. "They'd all wish they'd've known him. Talked to him. Cared more."

"They'd see him as a somebody, not a nobody."

Captain brought our drinks and we toasted.

"To Stan. The hero."

Bert gestured for me to write it all down. I scribbled on my pad: Stan playing with Charlie Parker, the war in France, marching with Martin Luther King in Selma, singing backup with Harry Belafonte on *Day-O*, being an extra in the movie *The Heat of the Night*.

It was getting late. Copy deadline was approaching. "I'll call it in," I offered.

"I'll do it," Bert said, lifting himself and shuffling to the bar. Snow masked everything out the window as he dialed.

As *I'll Be Home for Christmas* ended I heard my boss say, "Copy desk. Bert. Obit. Stanley Freeman. Age 62. Cook at Town Topic Hamburgers. No survivors."

He hung up, we put on our coats and stepped out. The world was covered in white.

Goodbyes were grunted. Bert pulled his hat low and walked away, down the street, into the silent night. His footprints quickly disappeared under the falling snow.

BACK HOME

It's like we're sitting Shiva
for this house.

Washing it.
Brushing away the cobwebs.
Turning out mouse droppings from
kitchen cabinets.
Lovingly tracing our brooms and cloths
over these empty floors
and walls
and cracked windows
that housed us for so long.

We will dress her,
put out some furniture
and a tea cup or two.
Not enough to honor her totally,
but enough to say "home" one last time.

They who will take her
have already seen her
as nothing but an anonymous corpse.

They've broken into walls and
busted holes in sidings,
looking for asbestos and other dangers
before they tear her down.

Doing their tests,
they've left a trail of coffee cups,
crumpled napkins,
and sharpie scribbles on the kitchen counter
—because they could.

We wash away the stains.
We repair the holes.
We cut the wild lawn and re-attach the hanging siding.
We will leave her
a clean and cherished corpse.

This slowly-cooling body
will protect us,
as a great beast,
which, though its heart is still,
yet gives warmth.

And in this familiar home
we'll lie
one last time,
and cry for her and us.

THE WILD GRASS

"I AM retarded."

"Don't use that word."

"Retarded! Retarded! Retard!" She kicks the weathered bench and I'm glad no other families are in the clearing.

"Please don't use that word. You demean yourself."

She kicks harder. I've got to distract her. "We should have picnics more often. Isn't it nice and sunny out here?"

"Hot and sunny was the forecast, Mama."

"That's what the weather man said."

"Hot and sunny all day long. Only not at night when the fireflies are out. They are mean. Always try to burn the house down, down, down to the ground."

She picks a scab on her shin. I want to remind her to pull her knee socks up so she'll stop her scratching those bites, but I don't. My lips press tight to keep from criticizing or controlling. It's so hard not to say anything.

Back of my neck is hot. Did I miss a spot with the sunscreen? Better not have missed on her.

A bee lands and swirls in her lemonade. She's occupied with her scab so I quickly splash the drink to the ground. The creature circles angrily in the wet dirt.

The sandwiches are growing stiff, their edges curling in the sun.

"You wanted a picnic. Aren't you hungry?"

She scrapes at lichen growing on the table. She'll get a splinter under her nail and that'll be the end of the day.

"Are we going to talk about the weather or not?" she asks.

"Yes, the weather. Some of us find it unseasonably warm today."

"And humid like a shower with the fan broken when I disappeared."

She's not forgotten that, when she couldn't find herself in the mirror.

"But you didn't disappear," I say. The minute it's out I regret it.

She leaps from the picnic table, running across the low-mowed circle and into the tall dry grass skirting the woods.

"Come back, there might be snakes," I yell.

She stomps knee-deep among the wildflowers. Pollen and hundreds of little creatures take to the air. Please don't sting her.

"Come back and have a sandwich."

The cicada's high drone is the perfect wrong sound right now. Can't they stop for five minutes? Can't everything stop for five minutes?

"We can take off the relish if it's not a relish day."

"Will the snakes bite if I step on them?"

"Please help me eat these, darling."

She turns to me, standing stiffly, legs hidden by the yellow weeds. "Who are you calling darling?" she asks.

"You're darling, sweetheart."

She takes a step backward. There must be a slope because the weeds reach her waist now. Why did we come here? We should have stayed home. We could have had a picnic in the backyard.

"Which is it? Darling or Sweetheart?" she asks, a challenge in her voice.

What is the right answer? What will bring her out of the wild grass?

She takes another step back. She's up to her shoulders, only a few yards from the darkness of the pines and who knows what's in there.

Don't let her see my panic. "Which do you prefer?" I ask, spreading a smile.

"I prefer. I prefer. When did I get that option?"

The sun on my neck is definitely burning. No matter how hard I try, there's always a place I miss and there's always pain because of it.

She takes another step toward the forest darkness, a disembodied head hovering over the dense field. Fear rises in my throat. This is a taste of what's to come.

"It's your choice. Darling—Sweetheart. Which do you prefer?"

"I prefer retard, Mama. Call me retard."

BUILDING A POND

I set about making a pond for the ducks.
Being practical to a degree,
I research on the internet.

I learn size: duck to gallon ratio.
I learn liner thickness, dimensions,
shelf height, vegetation, and filtration.
Having acquired enough knowledge,
I dig.
I line it.
I pull stones from the hills to create a
naturally haphazard coast line
around the edge of the hole.
Done.
Good job.
Time to fill it with water.

The pond fills—and
     the unexpected—
          the unforeseen—
               the magical—
                    occurs.

They say God is in the Details.
God is in the Details we leave out of our plans.

Sky, hill, rock, duck, dusk—all wobbling, wavering, warbling
—
A surface,
familiar but unexpected.
A new creation.

I forgot the Reflection.

IRREPLACEABLE

PAP, PAP, PAP. My sneakers smack the pavement as I run up Fifth Avenue. Traffic lights shine in the waning light. A city full of changing signals, but no one's here to notice.

Pap, pap, pap. Past Fifty-sixth. Fifty-seventh. A hedge fund lawyer in a three-piece suit darts out of the shadows and lunges, teeth bared. I don't even break stride. He'll never catch me.

Forget what you saw in movies or gleaned from books. Garlic doesn't work. Wooden stakes work but any stake will do. Crosses—don't bother. Daylight—yeah, they avoid that. As for the suave, well tailored, sexy trope, that's bull. Bloodsuckers have decaying flesh, random bits falling off, and stingingly putrid smells.

Yellow changes to red but I run through without looking. No cars to worry about. No bikes, cabs, or buses. The world is deserted.

Before the world changed, I worked at La Maison. Those aging society women decked out with jewels would call me *Um-Hello* or *Hey You* or *Boy*. The worst was the benefactress of the Metropolitan Opera and sustaining Angel at the Guggenheim. *Grande Dame* I named her. Her head pivoted on a wrinkled neck, searching for my lone dark face across the airy restaurant. Sometimes I'd hide behind one of the thick columns but with the many artistically-placed gold-leaf mirrors, she always found me.

"Um-Hello—" she'd sing to me, pearl-coated fingernails tapping the air, as her companions jangled their earrings and flashed toothy smiles. I'd move through the maze of tables, passing the gallery owners and their patrons, aging socialites and their interior decorators, gaggles of philanthropists' wives—catching snippets of conversations —"I found the latest exhibition at the MOMA less than stellar."—"We used to have a house in the Hamptons but with all the show people, the town just isn't the same."— "Shall we be naughty and have champagne?"—finally reaching Grande Dame. Eyelash extensions would flick to her water glass. It wasn't filled to the top. A half inch low. I'd tilt my head to acknowledge the command and go fetch.

They'd watch silently as I'd move around the table, refilling each glass to the correct height, careful not to spill a drop.

La Maison served upscale nouvelle cuisine; minuscule creations scattered delightfully akimbo across oversized plates. The ladies ate with pinkies raised, decorum that couldn't hide insatiable appetites. They never left a crumb or drizzled swirl. As I brought course after course—amuse-bouche, chilled soups, entrees, salads, petit fours, cheeses— the refined company only grew hungrier.

Was the first time accidental? I suspect not. Grande Dame shifted her ivory cane and caught my foot. I managed to keep the tray grasped in my hands, but the plates took flight. A solitary pomegranate seed rose, slowed as it reached its zenith, then descended, landing—a splatter of red—on white silk. Her blouse was ruined and Grande Dame pursed back the smile forming on her lips.

As china shattered on the marble floor, Marsha arrived. She bent low to Grande Dame, apologizing, promising reparations, and insisting I was to be immediately relieved of my duties. "He'll be gone before you finish your salad, Mrs. Sangdent."

"I wouldn't hear of it," the pinched lips curled. "I'm on the board of the Council for Enlightening Disadvantaged Youth. We must make extra efforts with these unfortunates. Diversity and such. I insist the young man stay. I'll see to it he learns to be more conscientious in his service."

And so, I became Grande Dame's personal affirmative-action condescension project. She didn't speak to me beyond securing my attention, then pointed out phantom crumbs on the linen tablecloth and invisible smudges on the wine glass. Grande Dame would invariably slide her designer shoe, luxury hand-bag, or endangered-species cane into my path and, although I came to expect these intrusions, sometimes she got the best of me. Something would fall. Eyes would turn. Heads shake. After several of these episodes, other luncheon patrons joined in. Oscar de la Renta shoes tripped me. Louis Vuitton purses sent my tray flying. The sound of shattering crystal mingled with tinkling laughter.

But, that was before.

It started as a news story happening somewhere else. People dying in some other hemisphere. Then our hemisphere but some other country. Then our country but some other state. The unstoppable spread closer, but not here in Manhattan. We went about our lives as if nothing would change.

But the ravenous hoard arrived. *The Infected.* The restaurant clientele diminished. Days of dwindling patrons. When Grande Dame failed to show for her longstanding reservation, Marsha phoned her. And I was summoned into Marsha's office.

"Mrs. Sangdent intends to maintain her relationship with La Maison, yet she prefers to be cautious," Marsha explained to me. "She won't be frequenting our restaurant until the crisis has passed. However, she desires our cuisine. She's ordered lunch and specifically requested you as server."

When the meal had been carefully packed in thermal containers, I was dropped at the Fifth Avenue address.

"Who is it?" the intercom asked.

"Delivery from La Maison."

I was sent around the corner and down the block, to the service entrance. This intercom asked the same question and I repeated my reply. The door buzzed open.

A dark-skinned beauty met me. I was about to say a line about her being worth the price of admission but her look made it clear: apart from color, we were not the same. Miss Superior gestured for me to unpack the food onto a silver cart. We took a service elevator—larger than my apartment —up to the top floor.

When the doors opened I rolled my cart behind Miss Superior and was led to an ornate dining room. Five Lesser Dames were seated around a table under a massive crystal chandelier. I prepared the plates and set one before each Dame and stepped back by my cart.

The meal progressed. The sun inched across the parquet floor, crawled up Chippendale chairs, slid over Waterford paperweights and under the grand piano. Arthritic fingers lifted roasted baby quails and sucked meat from tiny bones. Sounds of satisfaction and tinkling jewelry.

Grande Dame glanced at her champagne flute. I moved behind her to pour, careful not to let the Veuve Clicquot bubble over. As I stepped to the right, a Lesser Dame stuck out her foot. Stumbling, trying to keep the bottle upright, I slid on the parquet and crashed against the grand piano. There on the polished dark wood, a little framed painting on a golden easel wobbled and tipped forward, landing flat.

"Ladies, my precious objects!" Grande Dame screeched.

I straightened up. Not a drop of Veuve Clicquot had spilled. Reaching to restore the fallen miniature painting I—

"Do NOT touch that painting!" Grande Dame screamed.

The old woman hobbled across the room to the piano and reverently lifted the small framed piece back to its place of honor. Her jeweled fingers flicked me backward. "Stay away from this. It's *priceless. Everything* in this room is priceless. *Everything!* Except you."

My face flushed with blood, but I tried to keep it immobile.

"This is a Renoir," she snarled. "He's dead, which means there are a finite number of Renoirs and because of that, it is, unlike you, *irreplaceable*."

That was four months ago.

In the beginning, the killing went on night after night. People filmed it from rooftops and balconies, posting everything. Vigilantes tried to fight the Infected, but someone would get bit and turn. The homeless disappeared first. The poor next. The middle-class. The city emptied, leaving only the rich barricaded in their fortresses with their stockpiles and aides. Eventually their help went out in search of provisions and they got bit. I wish I could have seen those final privileged ones go down, each of them horrified that their wealth wouldn't save them. I imagine the Infected teeth piercing those necks, then spitting out the Botox clogging their incisors.

Now the city is empty. Even the pigeons and cockroaches are gone. Blood suckers are all that's left. Yesterday I saw a pack of wall street bankers searching for anything alive. They were easy to outrun.

But with the seasons changing and the days getting shorter, it's getting harder to find food before dark. Soon I'll be out of luck.

I listen for anything over the pap, pap of my sneakers down the middle of Fifth Avenue. Pap, pap is all I hear. I haven't seen another living person in weeks.

Does that mean no one's alive except me?

I might be the only one.

How could that be? I'm not special.

But now, maybe I am. Finally.

I'm one of a kind.

Ha Ha.

I push the Fifth Avenue intercom—the one in the front, not around the corner.

A guttural sound answers.

"Delivery from La Maison."

The door buzzes open. Miss Superior doesn't greet me. Nothing greets me but the smell of death and decay.

I take the elevator up. Blood smears the gilt mirrors. The doors open and pigeon feathers swirl as I step across the foyer to the ornate dining room. Chippendale chairs overturned. The chandelier lies shattered on the parquet floor—and there she is—in a red spattered gown, her white hair a tangled mat. Grande Dame's neck cranes forward, jewels glimmering over festering puncture wounds. She raises her nose and sniffs to check that I'm alive and full of blood. Smiles, showing yellow fangs.

"How disappointing. Still, in these difficult times, one can't be choosey," Grande Dame whispers. A strand of drool dangles from a tooth. "Come forward, Boy."

I shake my head.

Grande Dame takes a step toward me. "I wish there was a pigeon or something to help wash you down. Something to cut the taste of drinking *your kind*."

"There are no pigeons left. Or even rats." I stroll to the piano. Clumps of someone's grey hair and a bloody diamond earring grace the keys and the Renoir has fallen off its gold easel. "You and *your kind* picked this city clean. Drained every living thing."

She shakes her head, "Not every thing. There's you."

"I'm the last."

Grande Dame takes a step closer, "And you're mine."

I lift the little Renoir and run a finger across the painted surface. "You'll go out and find me food. Take care of me personally."

Grande Dame sputters.

"For a sip. No sucking. One *priceless* vial at a time."

She trembles with rage.

"You kill me and it's over. I'm the only blood left."

Grande Dame slumps, suddenly, incredibly aware.

Sinking into the overstuffed chair near the window, I kick off my tattered sneakers and lay blistered feet on the ottoman. Placing the little Renoir on my chest, I smile at her and silently mouth the word—Irreplaceable.

NATURE'S HUMOR

I had a little mulberry tree.
It had branches- one, two, three.
Upon its branches were green fruit,
getting large and sweet to-boot.

I would count the bounty growing.
Oh, fruit cuppeth over flowing!
Counted thirty on each branch,
They'd ripen soon. A day, perchance.

"No, they won't!" the birds did cry,
also squirrels squirr'ling by.
Sometime when I was not looking
all the berries they got to tooking.

Now I see the tree is barren.
Damn! From screaming I've got laryn-
-gitis. And my treat is null.
Should I try the birds to cull?

Yet their twitt'ring doth bring smiles.
Aye, the stuff of back yard trials.
Do I scheme to seal their doom or
laugh at Nature's sense of humor?

CREATION 101

TAKE YOUR PLACES.

Quiet down.

I'm waiting—

Okay, thank you.

We're going to cover the really important topic today, so pay attention. Take notes. This is a lab day so prepare to get dirty. Some of you may experience discomfort. I'm sorry, that's life.

Now, contrary to what you may think, we create VALUE before the VESSEL. Write that down. VALUE before VESSEL.

How do we create the value? Anyone? No one?

Okay, fine. Each recipe is different but they all have the same core ingredients. We will learn those before you get to improvise.

First, I will demonstrate and you will watch. Then you'll each get a chance to build your own.

As we go through the ingredients you must understand that I'm talking about ESSENCES not ACTUALS. Write that down. ESSENCES not ACTUALS.

When you hear Mozart, the music gives you ESSENCES, the notes on the page give you ACTUALS. When you think of dappled sunshine over a trickling brook in the forest, you are thinking the ESSENCE. The ACTUAL, the REAL exists, but it is nothing but the same-ol' atoms combined in different ways. Understand? The whole universe is nothing but the same-ol' atoms combined in different ways. Cat. Refrigerator. Star. Blanket.

So, first ingredient. Go on—write that down. FIRST INGREDIENT.

I take the ESSENCE of Gold. Notice I said Essence. This is not gold. It is gold EXPERIENCED. Today I choose that first nugget of gold found in Bodie, California in 1840 as it was reflected in the eye of the flabbergasted miner. You see? This gold essence is the foundation of the Soul.

Helpful hint—sometimes it's good to spit on your palm when you catch that essence so it will stick.

So far so good? To the gold essence we add the Essence of FIRE and EARTH and WATER and WIND. Write that down. FIRE and EARTH and WATER and WIND. Any idea why?

Anyone?

Okay, we add those for Energy, Stability, Fluidity, and Imagination. Pretty dull individual if one or more is missing. I've seen students skip one or more. Not good. Don't let this be you.

These are lightly stirred, not shaken. DO NOT SHAKE. If I see any shaking you will be asked to leave. It's not funny.

Once these are lightly stirred we reach the artistic part. This is where the improvisation comes into play as we are concocting what is colloquially termed the ORIGINAL PERSONALITY. (This is not to be mistaken for the ADULTERATED PERSONALITY which is created from the

Original personality getting mangled, battered, and deformed—and sometimes healed—over the course of a life.)

Understand? This will be on the test. ORIGINAL. ADULTERATED.

So, for today's example, I add seven spoonfuls of Wit and Mirth. That is a lot, I know, but still within legal bounds. DO NOT ADD MORE THAN TEN spoonfuls of Wit and Mirth.

Let's add a dram of Compassion and Empathy. More or less is okay, but you always need some. Do not neglect this ingredient or you get disasters.

I'm going to add one thimble of Athleticism, three of Visual Creativity, and four jumbo thimbles of Word-Play. You see what I'm doing? Makes you immediately interested, doesn't it?

But let's not stop there. I'm sprinkling in eight pinches of Unconventional Intellect. Fun, isn't it?

Once again LIGHTLY STIR.

Now. We let the mixture sit. It will quickly start to ferment. See? It's thickening. Expanding. When bubbles dot the top, blow across the surface to pop them and release the gasses. See? Did you see? Pay attention back there.

The mixture has altered significantly, hasn't it?

What does it remind you of?

Anyone?

It's become solid and has a dark rich brick-like color. Anyone?

I find it very close to the consistency of raw liver.

Okay, here is the important next step. You all washed, correct? Yes?

I'll wash again,—and when you are clean, you take a finger and prod the liver-like mixture. Watch.

There! Did you see that? Watch closely. I'll do it again.

See? It shimmers and shimmies. That means it's ready.

This is important, if you do not see it SHIMMER and SHIMMY, wait another few minutes. Should no shimmering and shimmying occur discard the mix and start again. DO NOT, I repeat, DO NOT CONTINUE if it doesn't shimmer and shimmy. This is important. It's not amusing or rebellious to continue. Don't do it.

Okay, now we have this liver-like solid that shimmers and shimmies.

Remember how I told you all to come to class without any breakfast? Did anyone eat or have water? Anyone? No lying or it's a bad thing. You must have an empty stomach. Okay.

So I didn't have breakfast or any water and now I'll swallow this whole. It will slide down easy, just breath normally and relax and it will go down okay. Don't chew. That's important. Swallow whole. Like—- *gulp*—that.

Once it enters, things happen quickly. You should feel movement increasing within your gut as the entity gestates and evolves. Keep it inside for as long as possible. I'm afraid this will be uncomfortable. This is the hard part of the process for us. Sorry. That's the way it is. Can you see? It is pushing against my skin and growing. Do not be concerned for yourself. It is only discomfort. Excuse me. It's—excuse me—it will—try to keep it down—it will—*cough*—claw its way—*cough*—up your esophagus and—*blat!*

That's always unpleasant. As I was saying, it will claw up your esophagus and beat against your teeth and when it does, you can expectorate it.

I see by your faces that this isn't what you were expecting. You didn't expect expectoration. Ha-ha.

Ha.

Okay.

So, we'll move on.

Set the creature on a clean flat surface to examine it. There should be no missing parts. Claws fore and aft, teeth above and below, limbs with enough heft, prominent gut, engorged heart, expansive mind. Do not skip this step. Use the checklist. Should there be any missing parts, you MUST expeditiously nullify and recycle. No sentimentality. As this one is intact I will not demonstrate the nullification. Usually one of you will have some missing parts in the beginning and we'll be able to go through that unpleasant process at that time. Another reason not to have breakfast.

Now that we have the soul, we need the vessel. That's the easy part: the sperm and egg. Humans create the vessels, we create the essence within.

This is where it gets fun. We can go with obvious vessels based on the ingredients we imbued in the soul, or we can choose unexpected juxtapositions. I'm into contrasts right now. So this witty, iconoclastically smart, compassionate soul will be placed in a diametrically opposite setting.

Let's scan the current opportunities. There's one that looks good in Ankara, Turkey. Here's another in Yokohama, Japan. Here's one in Kansas, USA. Let's check this out. The mother has serious anger issues. The father's brain vessel is weak so he'll be out of the picture soon. That'll make the family unit poor and mother will be even more angry. Poor, angry, and alone caretaker. That's a great contrast for this soul.

So watch now. Pay attention. As the sperm races to the egg, I hover over, cradling the newly formed soul. Any second now. Almost. Wait—-and BAM—egg and sperm meet and I dump the critter in. Perfect timing!

Poor fellow, he'll be so startled when he's born and finds out how little he has in common with his environment and family! It's fascinating to see how they cope.

Any questions?

Anyone?

Good. Now you try.

THE TOOTH FAIRY'S STASH

"MAAAAAHH!" Abigail screamed from her bedroom.

Folding the laundry, Catherine yelled back. "I'm busy!"

"It's an emergency!"

What the hell was the girl up to now? "What emergency?"

"I'm falling apart!"

Dear lord this child never gave her a moment's peace. "I'm trying to get these clothes folded. You're the one who hates the wrinkles."

"MAAAAAAAAAAHHHHHH!"

Catherine grabbed the pile of pink underwear and tiny t-shirts and stomped out of the laundry room.

"MAAAAAAAAAAAAHHHHHHHHHHHHH!"

Catherine headed down the hall to her daughter's bedroom. The one room in the house she hated. The girl insisted on having everything white and pink with unicorns and characters from *FROZEN*. It was so predictably cute it was disgusting.

Abigail was on the bed with her hands to her mouth.

"Okay, Abigail, what is it this time?"

"My tooth is loose!!" Abigail screamed.

"Not exactly an emergency," Catherine mumbled as she lay the folded clothes on the dresser.

"LOOK!" The six-year-old grimaced wide and pushed her pink tongue against the white nub in front. It arced back and forth on its hinge of flesh. "I'm falling apart!"

"No, Abigail, that comes much later. This is normal with baby teeth."

"I'm not a baby!"

"I'm not calling you a baby, I'm—" Catherine took a breath to stop herself from arguing with her daughter. "Listen, baby teeth fall out to make room for grown-up-girl teeth."

"When it falls out I get the Tooth Fairy?"

"If you put the tooth under your pillow and—"

Abigail jumped off the bed in a panic. "What if it falls out in the grass and I lose it? What if it falls behind the couch and YOU vacuum it? What if it falls out and I swallow it and it bites me in the tummy?!" Abigail stomped the floor and screamed, "I'LL NEVER GET THE TOOTH FAIRY!"

"Stop it! I've had enough of your screaming and stomping! I will take care of it now if you stop being so damn rambunctious! Okay? Wait here. Quietly."

Catherine stomped down the hall. This girl was getting on her last nerve. So relentlessly demanding. She had a mind not to leave anything under the pillow.

From her closet she grabbed her mother's ancient sewing basket. The woven fibers creaked as she lifted the lid. Up rose the smell of nights huddled at the kitchen table.

Catherine struggled with the arithmetic homework as Mama's quick fingers darted the needle through the cloth.

"No one wears out clothes like you. I don't know how you manage it. All I do is mend."

"Mama, what's twelve divided by—" the girl sucked her loose tooth—*"by four?"*

"Why are you making that sound? What are you sucking on?"

"My tooth is wiggly."

"Stop that sound. It's disgusting."

Catherine shook off the memory and carried the basket back to Abigail's bedroom. She moved aside a pink plastic unicorn with a glittery diamond collar and set the basket on the nightstand by the closet.

Catherine didn't sew but for the occasional loose button, so the basket still had all her mother's old wooden spools, ancient pin cushions, cards full of hook-and-eyes, and vintage rick-rack trim. Abigail peered at the assortment of antique sewing supplies. "Look at all this cool stuff! Can I have it?"

"Can we do one thing at a time, please?" Catherine asked, gritting her teeth.

"I'm going to take care of that tooth, Catherine. Can't bear to hear you sucking on it. Hand me a spool of thread."

Catherine's fingers grabbed the nearest spool. Pink. Of course. She turned her daughter's smooth cheeks toward the window to catch the light.

Mama gripped the girl's worried face and said, "Open your mouth and keep still."

"Open your mouth and keep still," said Catherine and she slipped the pink thread between the tooth and its neighbor, spun it around back and slipped out the other side. Slowly pulling the thread, she made a knot encircling the wobbly tooth.

Abigail's eyes widened in alarm. "You're going to pull? Don't pull! No!"

"It has to be done," Mama said as she tied the black thread around Catherine's tooth.

Catherine blinked, her chest felt constricted. A feeling of panic rose in her. "It—It—this is the way—it—" Catherine opened the closet door two feet.

"This is gonna hurt, girl, but I don't want to hear a peep."

Catherine shifted Abigail in front of the door, trying to hide that her hands were shaking.

Mama gripped her daughter by the shoulders and turned her to face of the open pantry. "You've heard of the Tooth Fairy, right?"

Catherine nodded, wary but hopeful. "Gives a present for the tooth?"

Mama leaned close, whispering in the girl's ear. "And you believe in the Tooth Fairy?"

A sob burst from Catherine, but she caught it, disguising it with coughs. She took a breath, "Abigail, tell me what you know about the Tooth Fairy."

"She's magic. And when you put a tooth under the pillow she comes riding into the room on her unicorn and reaches under the pillow—" As her daughter spoke Catherine carefully spooled out the pink thread, cut it, and tied the end to the doorknob with a drape of slack. "—and she takes the tooth and leaves a really wonderful present!"

Mama tied the other end of the thread to the pantry doorknob. "Tooth Fairy ain't comin' because—there's no such thing as the Tooth Fairy!"

Catherine leaned close to her daughter's ear. "Do you believe in the Tooth Fairy?"

Abigail nodded—vehemently.

A dull ache spread over Catherine. The Tooth Fairy doesn't exist. Unicorns don't exist. Life is brutal and full of pain and disappointment.

"Abigail, you're a big girl now. The Tooth Fairy—the problem is—"

"I'm going to take this tooth and hide it so you'll never find it. I'll keep every one that comes from your mouth and you will never be able to get them back. I'll own parts of you which will never be returned. Forever."

A fierce pain swarmed in Catherine. She'd never be whole. Her mother, long dead, still owned parts of her.

"Mommy?"

Catherine turned back to Abigail. The girl was waiting. Anxious. She patted Abigail's hands to soothe herself. "The problem is—the Tooth Fairy—the Tooth Fairy never knows when to look under the pillow. She gets frustrated looking when nothing is there, so she waits for a signal."

"What signal?"

"I only know one. Do you want to try it?"

"Yes!"

Mama took hold of the doorknob. "I'm going to rip that tooth out on three. One—"

The terrified girl squirmed.

"Stop shifting, damn it!"

"It has three steps. One—you stomp on the floor many times and be very loud."

Abigail stomped and stomped and stomped, her face scrunched in joy at being so loud and rambunctious.

"*Two—*"

"*Please, Mama—*"

"*Stop your whining!*"

"Number two, you scream 'Tooth Fairy' as loud as you can."

Abigail took a deep breath and screamed, TOOOOOO-OTTTTTHHHH FAAAAARRRRRIIIIIIEEEEEE!"

"Good job! That will really signal her."

"*Three—Get ready for pain—*"

"Three! Slam the door!"

Abigail rammed her arms forward—

WHAM!—

Catherine's Mama slammed the door—and both teeth went flying—*Catherine winced in pain*—and Abigail grinned, her new gap prominent, yelling, "We signaled the Tooth Fairy!"

"Let's look for your tooth."

"My tooth?" Abigail touched the spot. "It's gone!"

"Follow the thread." Catherine knelt on the floor as her daughter followed the thread tied on the doorknob. It led to the sewing basket.

"It flew inside!" Abigail pulled the thread and the basket tipped and—across the floor bounced buttons and spools and thimbles and ribbons and safety pins and—a little metal canister—the kind that used to hold camera film. The girl lifted it and gave it a shake. Many tiny objects rattled.

A smile spread across Catherine's lips. "My sweet girl, you found the Tooth Fairy's hidden stash."

WRITING THE BEAST

Writing.
It's kind of like—
You go after a wild or frightened beast.
You dart around, anticipating its moves,
cutting it off,
cornering it,
and try to rope it.
You yell and command it "COME!"
as it rears—eyes rolling.

You may capture it
(or find yourself face down in the dirt)
but you won't necessarily get to write/ride.

But sometimes
if you sit on a rock
with your back to the beast,
ignoring it,
doing other things,
the big animal will slowly
come up behind you,
nuzzle your ear,
and tell you its stories.

MOTHER OR OTHER

AS SHE DID every evening, Naomi phoned her mother with a mixture of hope and trepidation.

Ada answered with the usual, "I'm not dead yet."

"That's good, Mom. Anything going on?"

"Foxes came. Sidewinder. I need the regulars plus brewer's yeast, plain yogurt, and wheatgerm."

Naomi made a note. "Got it. I'll drive up tomorrow after —"

"Hiking tomorrow."

"It's probably time to think about stopping that—"

"Not happening."

"I'm worried about you all alone in those mountains. What if you fall?"

"My age, I'm liable to die anytime. Might as well go doing what I enjoy. My show's starting. Call tomorrow. If you don't get me, I'm dead."

And the phone clicked silent.

Naomi ran her fingers over the placemat trying to press out the wrinkles as the rush hour traffic honked by outside.

The next morning Naomi shopped for Ada, buying the usual healthy fare: lentils, whole grain bread, eggs, almonds. Nothing sweet, nothing adulterated with flavor. Utilitarian "fuel" for optimal transformation into energy. Naomi's mother didn't carry an ounce of fat and this echoed her personality as well.

Naomi thought of Ada hiking in the rugged mountains of the Eastern Sierras. *At eighty-seven years old, the woman should be cared for, not risking life and limb clamoring over rocks.*

As Naomi carried the groceries to her car, Ada had already been hiking for an hour and had reached a part of the trail where the path curved under a canopy of aspen trees. The fluttering yellow leaves created a tunnel of darkness. Within that tunnel was an unfamiliar shape on the ground.

Ada did not break stride. The creature in the path would surely scurry away when she neared. She marched on. The shadowed blob did not move. As she approached, the shape became visible. A deer—of sorts. It definitely *had* been a deer—Antlers, hide, hooves,—but this was not a normal corpse. It was a tumbled mess of fur and jumbled limbs as if someone had slipped out of a full-body-deer-costume and left it deflated on the ground. Save bone and bristly casing, whatever had been inside was gone.

The wind parted the leaves and sunlight illuminated a shimmering blur hovering over the remains.

Ada squinted at it. *A cloud of bugs. Dead animal. So of course bugs.*

The wind subsided and shade obscured the glimmering apparition. Not breaking her stride, Ada stepped past the deer left-overs and felt millions of tiny impacts against her body. No matter. They didn't sting.

At the peak overlooking a lake, Ada sat on a boulder to enjoy lunch. She peeled a hard-boiled egg and took a bite.

Her stomach revolted. It was as if a plunger rushed up to stop the egg from being swallowed.

I need to protein after this hike. But her throat was closed. Ada spit the egg over the cliff. She sat back to absorb the view but an itching started—not localized—everywhere. She knew better not to scratch, but it took all of her prodigious willpower.

When the discomfort became unbearable she started back. Downhill hiking was dangerous for someone her age. More chance of falls. She tried to be careful but she was so terribly antsy. Her clothes clung, chaffed, scratched, at every point they contacted her skin.

As she reached the last switchback down to her dirt drive, she started trotting.

This is stupid. You'll fall and snap your neck.

But she needed to run. Or scream. Every cell seemed to be angry. On the slope, she felt the momentum of her body getting away from her. She stumbled and grabbed the nearest tree, jerking herself back, face tangled in the branches.

Silly old fool, act your age!

Her isolated cabin was below and by clinging to trees, she managed to get home in one piece. She scrambled in, turned on the air conditioner and stripped.

Could she have touched poison oak or ivy? Was it even growing up here? Was it around those trees she'd clung to?

I may be half blind, but I know poison oak and ivy.

She opened the medicine cabinet and clawed through the mess, looking for a remedy.

What is that lotion? The pink stuff? Calamity. Calamity Jane. Calamity lotion?

The only pink stuff she could find was Pepto-Bismol and she had enough wits not to spread that over her raging skin.

Ada sat on the edge of the tub, lathering herself with lotion from a drawerful of mini containers taken from motels back when she still went out in the world. The phone rang, startling her. She answered, the receiver slick in her gooey hand. "You're early," she said.

"It's the usual time," said her daughter.

"How can that be?" Ada turned to the windows. It was getting dark.

"I guess you survived your hike."

"I'm alive, but something got me."

"Got you?"

The alarm in Naomi's voice made Ada smile. "Something itchy got me."

"Maybe poison ivy—"

"I know poison ivy when I see it. It was something else!"

Naomi's voice dropped, resigned to her designated role. "Do you have calamine lotion? I can get you some."

That's the name of the pink stuff.

"Get me that," Ada demanded. "My show is starting." She hung up, wriggled her feet into sneakers and went outside. She was naked but her cabin was far from everyone. Nearest town was twenty-six miles away. She'd chosen this isolated spot to be spared interactions with people and it had worked.

The sun dropped behind the mountain and that shadow spread across the long valley. Her "show." The sky transition from evening to night, bringing countless pinpricks to the blackness and just as many across her skin. It felt like something was squirming up one leg and down the other, curling between her toes, viciously nibbling at her.

What could this torture be?

There'd been that blurry cloud glittering over the path and she had hiked right through it.

I've got bugs.

Naomi drove up in the morning and as she unpacked the groceries Ada grumbled, "I don't think I can eat any of this."

"This is what you asked for!" Naomi said, sounding more annoyed than she'd intended.

"Well I don't want it! It's revolting! I can't eat ever since I went through the cloud."

"What cloud?"

Ada told about the cloud of bugs and how they shoved a plunger up her throat to stop her eating and how they were all over her and multiplying.

Oh lord. This is a new one. Naomi was used to her mother being an unreliable narrator. Ada believed odd things. Radiation from power lines, cancer from compact florescent bulbs. It was best not to argue. Naomi got out her reading glasses and scanned her mother's wrinkled skin. "I don't see any bugs," she said.

"Of course you don't," Ada snapped. "They're inside. They went through the skin. I feel them moving around."

"What would you like me to do?" was Naomi's go-to placating question.

"Look them up. Do research on your phone. Look up Cloud of Tiny Bugs."

Naomi followed orders. Unbelievably there were many entries. "There are tiny gnats called No-see-ums: Ceratopogonidae. A family of flies or biting midges, 1-3 mm in length."

"No-see-ums. A perfect name for what I have inside."

"They bite, but I don't see any information about them getting under the skin."

"I'll prove it to you," Ada said.

An hour later they were in an exam room. The doctor, peering through a magnifying light, studied Ada's blue-veined legs for a long time then straightened his back. "I don't see anything, but we can start you on a steroid for the discomfort."

Ada glared at the doctor. "Do a biopsy."

"Of what?"

"Cut out some bit of me. Stick it under a microscope. Send it to a lab. You'll see."

"Where do you suggest I cut?"

"Pick a spot. They're everywhere."

"I'm not going to cut a random sample—"

Ada lifted her keys and opened the Swiss army knife dangling from them.

"Ma'am, just a minute—"

A jab to her calf and with a twist she lifted a snatch of flesh as blood dropped onto the white tile floor. "Look! You see? Some flew out!" Ada covered the knife with her hand. "Quick! Get it into a jar or they'll all escape!"

The doctor glanced at Naomi demanding she get her mother under control. Naomi widened her eyes to dump the responsibility back on him. He gingerly tapped the bit of flesh from the knife into a urine cup, twisting the lid tight. "I'll have this tested, but I doubt we'll find anything out of the ordinary."

"Oh, you will. You saw them come out, didn't you?"

The doctor shook his head.

"Well, I did. They're small but they exist. They're called NO-SEE-EMS for a reason!"

An aide was ordered to dress Ada's puncture and Naomi followed the doctor out of the room.

"Your mother needs a complete mental health assessment. She may have Alzheimers. Sometimes it can affect a change in personality or moods. She seems quite belligerent. When did that start?"

Naomi looked down at her hands as if the old woman's behavior were her shame. "She's always been this way."

"Oh," the doctor said with some sympathy. "You should seriously consider putting her in a home." And he tossed the plastic cup with the bit of flesh into the hazardous waste bin.

On the drive back to the cabin Ada fidgeted and squirmed in the passenger seat, sighing heavily to indicate she was stoically not complaining. All the trip Naomi argued—with herself, her therapist, the doctor, and her mother. She couldn't send her mother to an assisted living home. No one would accept her. They wouldn't understand the woman's harshness. Naomi needed to bring Ada home to live with her. Of course her therapist railed against it, reminding Naomi that "you don't owe anyone anything." Naomi could only shrug.

As she drove up the dirt road to the cabin, Naomi took the plunge. "Mom, I was thinking, maybe it's time for you to come live with me."

Ada laughed. "Live with you? In the city? I hate people!"

"You wouldn't have to mingle," Naomi said.

Ada gestured at the cottonwoods, sage, and scattering quail. "Leave this? You're insane."

"I'd love to have you nearer."

"Who cares what you'd love, it's my life! You'll never get me down among the idiots."

Naomi nodded pushing back tears. Ada waved her hand, dismissing further talk and got out of the car. "You can stay or go. I'm taking a bath."

Ada filled the tub with hot water and as she slipped one foot in, she felt them panic. Her foot and leg shrunk as the creatures abandoned it, racing up to find refuge. She slipped the other foot in and felt the same exodus. *I'll drown them.* A thrill of vengeance and triumph flooded her. She added hotter water and she lowered her body below the scalding surface. All of her was aswirl with migrations. The population raced to her face.

"NAOMI! COME LOOK!" she screamed.

But her daughter was in the parked car crying.

Her head felt about to explode, swelling and puffing with the throngs of desperate bugs.

I've got you now.

She took a deep breath, submerged, and felt a mass of movement. The flurry of the doomed.

One. Two. Three. I can last. You can't.

They scrambled like mad—*twenty eight, twenty nine*—swirling away from her face, looking for safety—*forty six, forty seven*— scratching and clamoring—*sixty nine, seventy*—and then—nothing—no movement—not a tiny stir—stillness— *I got them!*

Bursting up, she gasped for air.

They attacked at once. Furious at her. Her whole body was scourged from within.

She tumbled out of the tub, screaming, scrubbing with the towel, "NAOMI! NAOMI!"

The door banged open and Naomi stared at her crazed mother, "What is it?"

"I don't know what they are, but they aren't bugs. These bastards are smart. They may be aliens. The iridescence wasn't glimmers off insect wings, it was glimmers off their tiny space ships!"

"Mom, you need to calm down."

"Look at this!" Ada put her hand into the murky tub water. "See!? They're all moving out of my arm!"

The old woman's skeletal arm looked as it always looked and Naomi was reaching the end of her patience.

Ada grabbed her robe and pushed past her daughter. "Come on! Get your phone. You need to research aliens."

Naomi had humored her mother about bugs, but spending the evening researching aliens was not gonna happen. She stared at her reflection in the bathroom mirror. *Leave now, you'll only get hurt.*

Naomi stepped out into the living room. Ada was putting a blanket on the small couch.

"What's going on, Mom?"

"Making a bed for you."

"You want me to stay?" Naomi asked with a little too much hope in her voice.

"We need to research and test. They don't like water, so what else don't they like? I'll win. I'll drive them away."

Naomi sighed. *You're probably right, Mom. You drive everyone away.* She collected her purse and keys. "I'll head home. I wouldn't want to catch your bugs."

"They AREN'T BUGS so you won't catch them! They're not looking to *move*. They *like* living in me." As she said that, Ada suddenly felt quite special. Special that they'd chosen her.

At the door, Naomi stopped. *The woman is old. She's going through some mental breakdown and needs sympathy.* She turned to face her mother, arms wide, inviting a hug.

Ada sneered. "Kissy-kissy again? I thought you were done with Hallmark propaganda."

This woman will never stoop to being warm or mothering!

Naomi had her fill. "Whatever the problem is, I don't care. I'm done. I won't be calling anymore. If you need something, get it yourself."

Naomi left and raised a middle finger in her pocket as she did.

The uncharacteristic departure didn't even register with Ada. She was excited about the creatures choosing her and hurried to the bathroom to stand naked before the mirror.

She squinted at her body. "Hello?"

Touched her chest. There was a movement in her and a warm glow moved to her sternum. A pressure, mirroring each finger and the palm, pressed back. They were touching from within. She patted her arm. A patting rose up, tapping in sequence to her. Everywhere she touched her body, it pressed back from within. A gesture of connection.

"You are welcome here," she said. "Take up residence. Make me your home. I'm yours."

A rush of activity sped through her and her itching ended instantly.

Ada imagined the creatures living in her. How did they manage, stumbling in her stomach, barreling through the blood, traipsing about the trapezius, lounging in her liver? Did they ever get to fly? Were the glitters wings or armor or space ships? Did they take vacations to her lungs and soar about the bronchial tubes? She swore she heard them scratching at her eardrum. When she looked at the bright sky, there they were, floating in the fluid of her eyes. When she coughed she searched for them, hurled into space before her. Minute shimmering specs that rushed back inside through nostril or skin. *Who knew skin was so permeable!*

That evening, Ada noticed her arm shaking as it lay on her lap. *What are they up to?* After a moment, her arm rose an inch and dropped. *They're making me move!*

She whispered to the mirror's reflection, "This is exciting—not to be in charge of my life. I'm proud to be your vessel."

Naomi went to therapy twice that first week. She knew to disengage was setting a healthy boundary, but it was torture. She could think of nothing but the fact she was abandoning her mother.

"She's the one who abandoned you," the therapist said. "That's why you're so desperate to get her love."

"I know."

Eight days later Naomi's phone rang. The caller ID of her mother. A jolt ran through her. Maybe Ada had been found dead by some hiker.

"Hello?"

"Sorry, daughter, requesting forgive," said a feeble voice on the line. Clearly Ada, but clearly not herself. The words were mumbled and the syntax bizarre. *A stroke?*

"Mom, are you okay?"

"We need help. Take us in with you."

"Really?"

Naomi listened to the hum from the phone. It sounded like snowflakes hitting glass. Tiny impacts.

"Time to be family."

This is an abrupt about-face, Naomi thought. *Could my definitive break have persuaded Mom that she needs me? Perhaps change is possible. Or maybe it's a stroke. Will it last? Does it matter? It's here now.*

"That'd be wonderful, Mom. I'll get a room ready for you and pick you up tomorrow."

"Good," the snowflakes tapped, and the line disconnected.

After a frantic morning getting the guest room ready as a studio apartment, Naomi drove to the mountains. When she entered the cabin, Naomi was shocked to see her normally thin mother looking like a skeleton. "Mom, have you been eating?"

The old woman mouthed something incomprehensible. Naomi decided to grab a few clothes and get on the road as fast as she could. Ada was clearly unwell.

"I'll come back here later for whatever you need. Are you okay to go now?"

Naomi watched her mother struggle to speak. The wrinkled jaw moved from side to side, mouth opened, dry pale tongue bulging. The tongue found shapes and lips formed words. A bit slurred, but Ada articulated, "We—happy—go."

She can barely talk. It's got to be a stroke. What's the test?

"Mom, close your eyes and stretch out your left arm and touch your finger to your nose."

Ada's eyes closed. Her left arm rose slowly, extended out, vibrating in a pulsing cadence. The elbow bent and the pointer finger docked with the nose. Ada opened her eyes and her lips boiled into a smile.

As they drove away Naomi touched her mother's arm. The old woman's skin seemed to rise to meet hers, but it was probably the jolting of the car. "I'm so glad you decided to come live with me."

"We need population," Ada whispered.

In her suburban house, Naomi showed Ada into the hastily modified guest suite complete with kitchenette. "You've got your own TV, fridge, microwave, bathroom, and a balcony to view the world. Your new show."

"Food."

Naomi offered several healthy soups from the cupboard but Ada shook her head to each. She pulled frozen Lean Cuisine meals from the mini fridge. Nothing was acceptable. "Sweet," Ada whispered.

Naomi slipped down to the kitchen and collected the stashed goodies she kept for emotional emergencies. Oreo cookies, gummy bears, red vine licorice, and Fanta. Ada's arms trembled for them and as she ate, she seemed to swell and gain color. Sugar was bad but if it brought her appetite back, it was worth it.

"How's the itching?"

"No itching."

"So the bugs are gone."

"No bugs. Only us."

For her own supper, Naomi decided on one of the rejected frozen dinners. Lean Cuisine chicken and rice. She peeled back the lid, set it in the machine, and pushed 4 on the microwave.

"AHHH. NO! STOP!" Ada screamed.

"What's happening?"

"MACHINE OFF, MACHINE OFF!"

Naomi turned off the microwave and hurried to her mother. "What—"

"Wave machine break—technology, scramble cells."

"What technology?"

"Our. Never use. Honor. Never."

Naomi promised.

"Good thankyous, child."

It's clear. Mom is succumbing to dementia. But, to be thanked and acknowledged as her child!—what a miracle! This could be the personality change from Alzheimers that the doctor mentioned.

Naomi bought all that Ada requested. Lucky Charms, gummy bears, Poptarts, Cocopuffs, and Fanta. What did it matter? The woman had been a health nut all her life. It was time to stop the regimen. Sugar became Ada's staple. She gained weight and her skin swelled.

Usually when Naomi knocked and entered, she found her mother watching soap operas on TV. Sometimes the woman sat by the sliding-glass door to the balcony, listening to the people on the street, sirens, and traffic, watching the world change from light to dark and back again.

Naomi always went in to say goodnight and Ada seemed to smile. Naomi felt the possibility of love from her mother for the first time in her life. She told her therapist, "I know she's not all there, but what is there is kinder than it ever was."

Three months drifted by. Ada grew quite round. She spoke little. Did less. One evening Naomi came in to say goodnight and found the room empty. Naomi tapped on the bathroom door and opened it. Ada sat on the edge of the tub, patting her arms, patting her legs, patting her face and hands and shoulders.

"Saying goodbye," she said.

"I came in to wish you goodnight," Naomi said, kneeling beside her mother.

Ada's hand rose slowly and moved to Naomi's cheek. A light caress. Naomi never knew such a touch from this woman. It brought tears to her eyes.

"Spilling," Ada said.

And Naomi nodded, smiling.

The next morning Naomi tapped on Ada's room and entered. Ada was standing by the closed balcony door. Her head hung at an odd tilt as she pulled on the handle. The door didn't move.

"I'll open that for you," Naomi said, hurrying to her mother's side. She touched the old woman's arm. The skin was cold and stiff.

Naomi bent low to look at her mother's face. The eyes were half open, dry, unmoving. Naomi put two fingers against the wrinkled neck. All she could feel was a vibration, a whirring under the frigid skin. No pulse.

Yet Ada continued to pull at the door. A jerky, awkward tilting, as if using the body's weight for momentum.

Naomi knew something was off, but she wasn't going to think about it. Her mother wanted to go out.

She reached under the clawing hand and clicked the lock switch up. The door slid open, causing the old woman to tip and, as quickly as the body tipped, it rose a few inches off the ground and righted.

The body began to swell beyond its already pudgy state. It expanded and expanded. Naomi took a step back from her inflating mother.

The wrinkled skin became like boiling oatmeal. Bubbles rose and popped, releasing millions of *things*, before the skin sunk and restitched itself. One mass after another, clouds of glittering nothings burst from the old woman, swirling, emerging from every part of her—through skin and eyes and mouth—and as they poured out, the woman's body shrank, deflating, until it collapsed in a heap of skin and jumbled limbs, an abandoned Ada costume.

The cloud of shimmering billions swirled and split in half. One mass hovered as a blur, flashed bright green, and tornadoed out the open door, splintering off in every direction. The other half coalesced, glittering into a shape— arms, legs, torso, head—

The phantasm took a floating step—with a disconcertingly familiar shuffling. The shimmering visage moved as one, a fluid compilation taking another step toward Naomi. And another. The tiny glittering bits coalesced into Ada's face—smiling, motherly, welcoming. Arms rose, outstretched, and beaconed. "Come, sweetheart," toned the vibrating form.

Naomi felt the tug in her heart. If she stepped forward she'd get that hug she'd always wanted.

Naomi stepped forward and swerved around the phantasm to the kitchenette. She pushed *ten minutes* and the microwave whirred.

A civilization screamed as the visage of Ada disintegrated into millions of flashing fragments, swirled past the balcony, and disappeared. The few remnants of what had been Ada floated to the floor.

Naomi got out the broom and dustpan.

DO IT YOURSELF POEM

This poem may
fall apart in five years.

I didn't construct it to code

or consult with the experts.

I just put it up
for the shade.

ASHES, ASHES, WE ALL FALL DOWN

SOME SAY DEATH brings people together. My brother and I have been working hard at staying apart, so the intrusion isn't welcome.

Emailing is my preferred method of communication but I know a call is de rigueur for this kind of news. It takes a few days to get around to it as death is time-consuming, but I finally phone Ralph to tell him about Mom, relay that the ashes are imminent, and suggest the place I've been looking at.

"It's one of those cemeteries with the crypt-drawer-thing in a wall where the remains are stored."

"Internment," Ralph says in a tone to make me the bad guy.

"Mom and Dad could be put in there together," I suggest.

"So you still have Pop."

My lack of answer is an answer. Dad is in the closet in a bronze urn behind shoeboxes of photos.

"You kept him thirty years in the closet. Why don't you keep 'em both there? Shove 'em in the back behind the old thin-clothes you're sure you'll fit again some day."

I remember why I haven't been in touch with my brother for years. "Let's just take them to the cemetery I found, say a few words, and try to make it special."

"Sure," he says uncharacteristically. "Only let's bring 'em by Red Maple first."

"The roads are probably still snowed-in that far out."

"I'm sure they're plowed by now."

We argue until I let him win and agree to meet at old homestead.

The roads have indeed been plowed since the blizzard and I make good time. Mom is in a cardboard box in the passenger seat, Dad in his urn beside her, seatbelt securing them both.

I get there first and stop the car beside the same mailbox with the different name. The driveway to the big old house is hidden under an untouched blanket of white. 43 Red Maple Road, where Mom and Dad were young lovers, where Ralph and I grew up: skinned knees, swinging tires, broken teeth, wet mittens dangling from cuffs. Nostalgia stings my eyes.

The trees are a lot bigger but leafless so I can see the house well. It's been painted. Still the same wide porch and glowing windows. His-and-her SUVs fill the carport. Two kids burst from the door with a huge red dog. Typical screaming and barking ensues. Hopefully, they won't pay attention to the hovering woman parked on the road.

Ralph pulls up, his car scrunching snow behind me. He looks middle-aged; wide, bearded, and balding. When did my brother get so old? How do I look to him? I dismiss the thought.

"Hey, Ralph."

"Hey, Sis."

We hug like football players on opposing teams.

"Got the folks?'

I nod to the passenger seat.

Ralph spreads his arms, taking in the house. "Mom'n'Pop would want to visit the place. Gotta see 'home' afore you're interned."

"I wish you'd stop using that word. It makes it sound like they'll be in prison. They'll have a plaque. A location we can visit. A clean well-lighted place."

Ralph ignores me and opens my car, lifting the cardboard box that's Mom. I haven't opened it, but there he is, peeling the tape, pulling up the tabs, un-doing the baggie's twist tie. I have to look. She's the same gray sand as Dad, only not as coarsely ground. Grinding must have gotten better over the years.

"Here." He hands me Mom and reaches in for Dad.

Ralph lifts the top off Dad and peers in. "We should mix them together."

"Not a good idea. Are we done here?"

Ralph covers his mouth like he's having a feeling so I turn away to give him privacy and a red barking blur bounds toward us—leaps—paws knock me—space upends —and inertia does the rest. Mom flies—up—over—open— down—a swath of gray ash across white snow.

Ralph does a man-voice I've never heard before. "BAD DOG!"

Rover runs, ruffing at Ralph. Paws strike. Dad becomes airborne—tips—spills—a miniature storm cloud—and crash lands.

The furry interloper sniffs the sprinklings, licks once, and races off.

No. No, no, no.

I feel sick.

This can't have happened.

Mom and Dad are scattered Jackson-Pollock-like across the snow.

My stomach wrenches and I clutch myself, unable to breathe as Grief and Death and Loss kick inside.

Ralph covers his mouth, eyes wide. He must be holding back sobs. Or could he be laughing? No, it must be sobs. My little brother needs me to be strong. Got to buck-up and deal with this. I swallow the tears and press the pain down.

"It's okay, Ralph. This is not that bad. Could be worse—could be summer with grass and dirt and worms. We're lucky. They're on the top of clean, fresh snow. If we scoop up the layer, we can collect them, take them somewhere to melt, let the water evaporate, put them back in the boxes, and they'll be fine. I'll take care of everything."

I pop the trunk to search for a tarp, a cooler, anything to hold the ashen snow. Three plastic grocery bags and ice scraper should do.

WHAM! Something cold and hard hits the back of my head.

I turn. Ralph is already packing another in his hands.

"What are you doing!?" I yell—but he pitches and it splats across my chest. Bits of slush and gray ash dangle from my jacket.

He stands waiting. So familiar: the arms wide, the taunting smile, the teasing eyebrows, his hips moving in the *dare-you* dance.

"Don't be a jerk!"

He sticks out his tongue and bends to scoop more and I can't allow this. I stomp past Mom and shove him. He lands butt-deep, grinning, displaying that old broken tooth.

"This isn't funny!" I insist.

Ralph flops flat, surrendering.

I get to the task at hand. Make an indentation in the snow and prop a grocery bag open in it. The scraper mows a layer of ashen flakes, clearing a white swath in the gray. Carefully tipping the precious load into the impromptu urn, I return for another long scraper-full. "See? This will work. Just don't move."

Shouldn't have said that.

Still prone, Ralph swings his arms up and down, legs open and closed, smearing Dad under his boots. A snow angel with a filthy gown.

"Stop it!"

"Or what? You'll tell Mom?" He dredges his hands, scooping up Dad, and smacks him round.

I fling the scraper-full at him. Ash and snow hit his face.

"HA!" I shout triumphantly.

"Got you," he laughs, hauling himself upright and brushing bits from his eyes.

Did I just lose?

Gray mess surrounds me. There is no collecting this.

I grab a handful of Mom, scoop up a wad of Dad, pack them tight, and shoot that icy ball of parents *hard*. Ralph dives but gets nailed in the shoulder.

"Take that, creep!" I yell. "I'll pulverize you!"

"You and what army?!"

Game on. Balls fly. Snow explodes. Ice and ash go down my shirt. Ralph has parent-crusts in his beard. Vapor clouds snort from us both. The dog returns, chomping on all he can fetch. The two kids join in and it's like the old days with squeals and joy and footprints and victory and freezing and laughter and falls mixing everything. Ralph and I get the idea at the same time and start rolling snow, making the large balls, lifting one on top of the other. Bottom, belly, head. Sticks for noses.

It's twilight when we wave to the children called in home. As they depart for supper, Ralph and I stand holding hands and bumping shoulders in front of the two gray "snowmen."

Mom and Dad will melt in the spring.

DESERT ENTRY

God is alive and well and living in the desert.
There, from every burning bush he is found
giving vast orations in the brassy click of insect wings.
Above his chattering,
silence stretches over the mammoth boulders
which fell before I arrived.

Oh, you could drive me into believing in you
if you had me to yourself for a while.

Spiked plants laugh at the flesh I carry on my limbs.
And indeed, I am a laughable sight
in God's land of twisted forms.

Raucous heat and stone and scrub and snake,
which scorch and trip and tear and hiss,
surround me for miles with active indifference.

You were not made to bow or bend
and have every right to sneer as I carry my soft body into
your sandy gut.
Shall I enter to find out how expendable I am?
How better fit is your lizard
and your Juniper,
flourishing in a grotesque laugh.

All of you is a laugh.
A laugh of being twisted, thorny, toxic, and dry.

Reason is left at the edge and you find me nodding,
wide-eyed in supplication
at your irrefutable perfection.

I am converted.

WELCOME, C'MON IN

THE BEGINNING CAN BE pointedly precise or obliquely obtuse. After all, it's hardly more than a greeting.

Dangle the bait. Hook. Reel in slow. So slow you don't even feel the pull.

I'm no expert but I've caught a few. Would have mounted trophies if that were possible.

Wording is the thing. Easy going. Easy flowing. Friendly-like. Adding a smidge of slang to put folks at ease.

Most don't even notice the words I sprinkle for the subconscious. *Red* is common but I like to thresh it up with surprises. Like *thresh*. Gives a sense of danger. Danger draws you in. Gives zest to cozy lives. Makes you wonder— *What is going on?!*

Sometimes I set out pedestrian things. Everyday items.

Spoons.

Or a cheese grater.

The captive mind leaps into action. *What will be done with these!? A cheese grater?*

Basement. Sounds of something dripping. Flies circle under the glaring bare bulb. A cheese grater is removed from a worn leather satchel. The cheese grater inches closer. Near a most tender part. It hovers over bare skin and then—

Can you see it?

Where does it gravitate to? What can it toy with? Images fly. The forbidden. The unthinkable becomes visible behind the eyes.

Can you see it?

The swinging bulb seems brighter. Muffled voices echo. What's being done with this cheese grater? *You know.* Something disturbing.

There's a terror there. Down in your gut it rumbles, in that hidden place. It isn't me. It's you.

Every time you see a cheese grater, remember what you imagined.

I offered the seed. You did the rest.

I'm not a bad sort. I don't make you feel anything I haven't felt. I've done it all to myself. Everything.

I know if I push too hard I lose you. I've lost a few by going too far. So let's stop now and move on. To spoons perhaps?

I call forth great geese to fly you on their smooth muscular backs feathered in brown and cream. A wide V formation of determined companions all heading— somewhere. They fly, calling out over the green and gold patchwork below. You're with them, surrounded by them.

Listen to that honking!

Listen to the great wings *thresh* the air.

Listen to the chimes.

Chimes?

There, behind,—

—tied to the black webbed feet with red ribbons

—dangling in the wind

—spoons.

The spoons chime together as bells, ringing out to churches underwing. Bidding the church-bells join the joyous cacophony.

And? What next?

Well—if the satin ribbons are frayed or brittle with age, they might break. They might break and release the spoons and there is no telling where those might land.

Perhaps the spoons plummet, tarnished bowl-head first, and splash in that pond below, zig-zagging past algae and green bubbles to silently stop on the silty bottom.

Can you see them?

Down there, nibbled on by curious tadpoles.

This might not go further.

Let's rewind.

Perhaps the ribbon breaks and the spoons drop in a slow arc to the landfill. They land in the landfill and they plop atop the favorite photograph. *Why is this favorite photograph in the landfill?* A photograph that didn't mean to be discarded but got mixed up with the junk mail when— *when what?*—when the grandchildren knocked everything off the mantle.

Can you hear the crash? The anxious cries?

The spoons frame the precious discarded black and white picture of—

You can almost see it.

Of—

—the departed father.

A derby-hatted man—who's almost smiling. A man who almost never smiled is almost smiling—and amidst the cawing gulls, *we're at a landfill remember,* amidst the cawing gulls—only *you* see—the spoons and cherished photo become covered by the last truckload of trash, not to be seen again for one hundred years.

Not long enough?

Not to be seen again for a millennium!

And in a millennium they are uncovered by—let's say by future archeologists! Discovered, and methodically uncovered by future archeologists trying to get a clue as to what went wrong. What went wrong with—

No. Let's rewind.

The ribbons break. The spoons tumble through clouds down to that suburban home, there—the last one at the edge of the development. And as the sun heads for its bed, the spoons hit the roof, clatter and clang on the tiles, bouncing like goats down a hillside, skipping off to land noisily on the front step—just as the teenage boy, his courage finally summoned, taps on the door.

And so?

The two ribbon-tied spoons glisten at his feet.

And so?

This is not the greeting he expected.

And so?

This is not the greeting he expected but he picks up these spoons, these gifts, and when the teenage girl opens the door, he presents them. The two watch the flock honk overhead, and because they both are aware that her parents have left for the evening, she accepts the spoons and, barefoot, leads him to the kitchen when—

When what?

—when all across the county the power goes out.

Perhaps a goose landed on the lines.

And in the surprise darkness of the kitchen, the girl pauses her walk but the boy doesn't, and the accidental bumping becomes a fumbling which becomes a quickening of hearts and unseen reddening and neither knows what to do but they make it up as they go along.

And maybe the naked boy licks one of the spoons and slides it over the naked girl. And maybe she guides him and they do things with the spoon because they're artists at that moment and in a state of grace, without shame to halt their inspiration.

And only you know what they do with those spoons.

And the next morning their respective Moms and Dads talk about the power outage. As Dad *grates cheese* into *threshed* eggs they talk about emergency kits and flashlight batteries. And in their respective homes the boy and girl lift sacred spoons with cereal or yogurt and smile at their secret.

And you know their secret. You made it.

It could end there. Or there could be a coda of sorts.

Perhaps—no one understands why they give spoons to each other on every anniversary. Or why their wind chimes are made of spoons hung from red satin ribbons. Or why they always look up at the honking V of geese and touch fingers. Or why, well into their eighties, the wrinkled hand of one slides a cool spoon gently over the blue veins of the other.

But you know why.

If a spoon falls from a goose or a cheese grater shines in a basement and no one's there to read it, did it happen? Does it mean anything?

Without you, these are just squiggles of ink on a page.

HOPE IS A THING THAT'S MOLTING

IT'S EIGHTEEN DAYS into our tenth wedding anniversary driving tour. We've seen Gettysburg and Valley Forge and ventured north to enjoy the Stafford Motor Speedway and the thrills of the Springfield Armory National Historic Site. Our next attraction was to be the Thunderbolt Mountain Coaster but we got waylaid by the storm and spent the night in this Red Roof Inn near Amherst.

In the office lobby as the motel coffee brews, I stare at the rack of local attraction brochures.

Dwight's doing pushups to CNN when I return. I hand him a coffee and brochure. "This looks interesting."

"Of all the attractions, you pick this?"

"Writers need to be around other writers. We get courage and inspiration from them."

"Since when do you write?"

I could remind him of the poem I published when I was in college and of my many carefully composed Amazon reviews that are regularly rated as helpful. "I have written and am thinking of starting again. This would mean a lot to me."

"You've never mentioned Emily Dickens in all—"

"Dickinson."

"Whatever. You've never mentioned her in all the years we've been married."

"I don't mention a lot of things."

I sit on a cement bench as Dwight parks his SUV and buys our tickets. I'm quite excited. It's been a long time since we've done something I wanted to do.

An artistic woman approaches. We're in Massachusetts so everyone looks artistic. She has a neck scarf and beads in her hair. She gestures to the bench. "Are you holding this for anyone?"

I glance up—Dwight's still by the ticket booth, swiping his phone. "No," I dare.

She sits and leans close. "Hope is a thing with feathers."

What am I supposed to say to that? Is it code?

"My favorite Emily poem," she says.

My face flushes and my fingers instantly fumble to spin my wedding ring. It's an annoying habit, according to Dwight.

"What's your favorite?" the arty woman asks.

"Too many to say," I mumble.

I don't know why people have to memorize and quote lines from poems. Actually, I haven't read much Dickinson. I know I read some in high school. What I remember is how she spent her life writing and didn't show a speck to the world. And wasn't she reclusive? Or at least, there was something about her not leaving home.

The guide arrives and the minute I step through the door I feel Emily's presence. She lived here. She wrote here. Just seeing this place can tell—she's my favorite writer!

I wedge through the crowd and lean over the velvet rope to view the parlor. It's so perfect! Elegant, but cozy at the same time. I can almost see Emily sitting on that tufted Victorian chair. Or reading by the fireplace. Maybe there's a dog, with soft brushed fur, curled on the settee.

"Ugly paintings," Dwight mumbles in my ear.

I don't say a word. I'll pretend I don't know him.

The delicate clock on the mantle chimes. What a thrill! She must have heard that a million times. Emily wound this clock then turned to gaze out this window, watching a horse-drawn carriage clip-clop by, completely at ease with being alone and apart from the throng.

The tour guide blocks my view. "In this parlor Dickinson's parents would receive guests, read the evening paper, perhaps needlepoint was done, a common practice among young women of the day. Those in front, please step back so others can get a chance."

Dwight quickly retreats. I keep my spot in front but press myself against the doorjamb to be considerate. Did Emily ever press against this doorjamb? Probably not. I don't press against doorjambs at home.

"Let's move on. We're going to see the second floor and I know you're all looking forward to a certain room. Keep together."

The group heads upstairs. Dwight waits for me but I wave him on and pause to separate us, touching the banister. My hand slides along the smooth wood. *Her hand slid on this!* As I rise, I imagine stepping up to my room. Stepping up to write my own private thoughts in my own private space.

On the second floor we're teased with the parents' bedroom, the father's study, the nursery, and now the maid's room. The guide drones on describing someone none of us cares about. He's doing it on purpose.

I spin my wedding ring. Dwight elbows me and hisses, "Stop fiddling. You look jittery. Maimey was never jittery."

Yes, I know. Maimey was full of gumption. All of Dwight's ancestors were full of gumption and I'm have none. Do I twist Maimey's ring to have gumption rub off on me?

The tour guide mumbles something. I turn around and everyone's down the hall! Hurry to them but I'm in the back. I'm in the back and it's Emily's bedroom! All I see are fanny packs and sweat stains. Dwight's right at the front! The tour guide says something about "Miss Dickinson's writing desk" and "poetical inspirations." I'm missing everything!

"You will find postcards, books of her writings, t-shirts, keychains, and many more souvenirs of your visit in the gift shop. Thank you for your attention."

The crowd pushes past me anxious to get mementos, Dwight points downstairs and as he passes, I rush to the velvet rope. *Look! Her room!*

Beside me is that artistic-looking woman. We both lean in, absorbing everything with reverence.

The deep mahogany sleigh bed. *Her head rested there! She gazed out of those tall windows!*

The woman points at the small perfect desk, on it a piece of paper, an ink well, and nib pen. "Where it all happened," she whispers.

I nod. She pats my arm and leaves.

This was where Emily worked and slept and was able to be alone. Able to be herself.

Tears surprise me and I spin Maimey's ring and—I'm not sure how, perhaps the twisting has widened the ring, but whatever the reason, the band of gold slips off and bounces under the velvet rope and rolls across the ancient floorboards. It rolls the width of Emily's bedroom and circles to a wobbling stop under her writing desk.

I look down the hall. No one's there. Duck under the velvet rope. Tiptoe across the room. Crouch, retrieve the ring, and slip it back on. I touch the desk. Touch her nib pen resting beside her inkwell. Tears come as I slide the pen into my purse. *I'll take good care of you!*

Back under the velvet rope, back down the stairs, my heart fluttering, and I'm dizzy with joy. My life will be so different now. I'll make a space for my own desk. Maybe in the garage. I'll get an inkwell from the right era on eBay. I'll write. My feelings will pour across the pages.

Dwight's in the gift shop, buying a sodas and snacks. I move beside him.

The pretty young cashier rings up the items. "Like the tour?"

"Her furnishings aren't exactly my taste," my husband says.

"Oh they aren't her furnishings. After the Dickinsons died, the house was bought and sold, rented, gutted, modernized, and when it was finally turned into a museum they decorated it to have that old-timey look. There are some original pieces but who knows what. Can I get you anything else?" the cashier asks.

"One of those. My wife fancies herself a writer." Dwight gestures to the container beside the register. The container full of nib pens. Nib pens exactly like the one in my purse.

"I'll be outside," I mumble and stumble through the doors into the glare.

I feel sick.

Everything's a sham. A show. You can tell yourself something is real, try to hold it, but it's pointless. "Poof. Gone."

A gentle touch on my arm. "Are you alright?" The artistic woman. "Something's gone?"

I don't know how to explain it.

"Your ride? An Uber? That happens. I'm that red van, far end. I can give you a lift."

I glance to the shop. Dwight continues chatting with the cashier. A shudder rolls over me and things loosen inside with the shake. "I'd appreciate that."

I follow her as we sidle between cars in the crowded lot. Something is happening. Something hopeful. "What was that line?" I ask. "Hope is a thing—"

"—with feathers," the woman says.

We near Dwight's SUV. Passing it, I put my hand on the hot roof and leave behind Maimey's ring.

"Hope is a thing that's molting."

PREVIOUSLY PUBLISHED WORKS

- SOMETHING BROKE published in *GONE LAWN* - 2014
- DINING ALONE ON VALENTINE'S DAY published in *FURIOUS GAZELLE* - 2014
- SUICIDE WATCH published in *THE MAGAZINE OF FANTASY AND SCIENCE FICTION* - 2018
- MUSIC THEORY published in *INDEPENDENT INK MAGAZINE* - 2014
- AFTER CHRISTMAS TURKEY published in *BLACK HEART MAGAZINE* - 2017
- THE KID - published in *SMOKY BLUE LITERARY AND ARTS MAGAZINE* - 2016
- SUMMER OF HOPE published in *BLACK HEART MAGAZINE* - 2017
- OLD DOG, NEW TRICKS published in *SMOKY BLUE LITERARY ARTS MAGAZINE* - 2016
- THE WILD GRASS published in *THE COLLECTION OF FLASH FICTION FOR FLASH MINDS* - Anchala Studios - 2018
- WELCOME, C'MON IN published in *DOES IT HAVE POCKETS* - 2024